Praise for *Coven: The Scrolls of the Four Winds*

"I wanted to let you know how much I thoroughly enjoyed reading your book *Coven*. It was well thought-out with people, plots, etc. You ended the book terrifically! The insight and information from chapter 13 onward was unmistakably brilliant! Truly. Loved the ending... leaves the portal door open to another book... maybe? You really added dimension to the tale in more ways than one. Kudos!!! When I was at the meet-up, I told them I was reading your book and thought they all should buy a copy because it was that good. Hell, it is awesome!!! Thank you Diane for such a fascinating and delightful book! You did a fabulous job."

—Linda S., Fox Chase, PA

"*Coven* was wonderful right to the very end and what surprised me most is that the whole time reading it, I was enjoying the story and failed to see that by the time I was through, I was actually learning valuable lessons, you tricky witch! I can't wait for the next book, I'll be running to the computer to get that as soon as it's available. I told my husband that I could see this book as a movie, like the Harry Potter adventures."

— Kelly Withers, Niverville, NY

"I finished your novel last night! I LOVED IT! It really took me to another world as I read it. Really! I found myself getting anxious for the heroines too, which is a commentary to your excellent character development. I really enjoyed the experience! "

—Nila S., Dallas, TX

"I read your book in a day—couldn't put it down! Loved the characters, the imagery, and the wealth of knowledge all wound into a spellbinding story. Congratulations! It is very, very well done!!"

—Suzanne K., Lower Merion, PA

"*Coven* was fabulous and hit many personal experiences head on. It is a relief and exciting to not feel alone in these."

— Carrie Aitken, Broomall, PA

THE SCROLLS *of the* FOUR WINDS

DIANE WING

Modern History Press

Ann Arbor, MI

ISBN 979-8-89656-050-0 hardcover
ISBN 978-1-61599-173-0 paperback

Library of Congress Cataloging-in-Publication Data

Wing, Diane, 1959-
Coven : the scrolls of the four winds / by Diane Wing.
p. cm.
ISBN 978-1-61599-173-0 (pbk. : alk. paper) -- ISBN 978-1-61599-174-7 (ebook)
1. Witches--Fiction. I. Title.
PS3623.I652C58 2012
813'.6--dc23
2012031007

Published by Modern History Press, an imprint of
Loving Healing Press
5145 Pontiac Trail
Ann Arbor, MI 48105

Tollfree USA/CAN: 888-761-6268
www.ModernHistoryPress.com
info@ModernHistoryPres.com

Distributed by Ingram Book Group (USA, CAN, EU, UK, AU)

Dedicated to all who believe

Also by Diane Wing:

The True Nature of Tarot: Your path to personal empowerment

Thorne Manor and other bizarre tales

Foreword

A Coven of Purpose and Integrity

I believe the "right" books come into our lives at the right time. Whatever you are reading, feel its energy and see how it corresponds to your own life. So it happened, and I am not in the least surprised now though it did take me by surprise at the time of happening, that Diane's book came to me just a week before I myself had to deal with unwanted energies and loose ends in my own life. And yes, it was something way more than a box with photos from the times long gone.

Reading the book, I was reminded of the value of grounding and psychic protection; more than just reminded, I was taught how to do so, and taught in the very relaxing and conversational manner which is lacking, often, from the "ritual" of teaching. I learned basic principles of Magic: the energy you give out returns to you three times multiplied; the wisdom and answers are inside our own souls and we just need to get access to them and magic can help us clear that pathway along with the prayer; food and lifestyle alters our vibrations and much more.

Through the journeys and struggles through time, space, emotions, and energies of the four girlfriends who also are sisters in Spirit and Keepers of the Scrolls of the Four Winds, I was reminded of basic and simple truths that each of them was exposed to and shared with the rest of the world at the end of the book. For example, Alexis, through the Gateway of the Element of Water, received a message which contained the following part that I found to be very true for myself:

> "Emotional reactions reflect issues that must be addressed within the self. Maintain power by controlling your own reactions. The actions of others cannot be controlled, but your reaction can be. You are responsible for your feelings. Being overly sensitive creates limitations. Approach life from a centered position and see the world with a more objective eye."

Love, gratitude, friendship, discernment, sincerity, and bonds of physical dimension on the callings of our eternal Soul. You will find it all in *Coven*, a book written with simplicity that draws your full attention to the luxury of the message, contained in between its pages.

By now you must be wondering if this book helped me to resolve that issue in my life I mentioned in the beginning... while this novel did not teach me the fine details, it did help me to learn that there is nothing to be afraid of if you know the rules, follow them, and approach life and all around you with love and gratitude for the lessons received. Diane Wing took the scary part of magic out and showed that there is nothing impossible for those with integrity, discernment, and a couple of other "right" tools, all guided by the loving soul, always in the search for ways to learn and grow. ...indeed, I might as well read a couple of other books about Magic :)

Victoria Evangelina Belyavskaya,
columnist for *Georgia Today*

Victoria
Amira
Earth

N

W

Alexis
Mina
Water

E

Cassandra
Iman
Air

S

Macy
Uzma
Fire

Prologue

Mesopotamia, City of Ur, 371 A.D.

Qadir stood defiant before the Council, awaiting their verdict. His floor-length black robe, belted at the waist, created a dark vortex amidst the white stone of the floor and walls. He felt no remorse for calling demons against his rival, Hamid, as they vied to be the Temple's next High Priest. Through this display of power, he showed the Council command of the underworld and his affinity to their patron, the moon god Nanna-Sin, who decreed the fate of the dead.

The crowd waited in silence to witness the judgment. In the balcony above them was Qadir's student, Amira. Strikingly beautiful with long black hair, her dark eyes watched her teacher's bold display of rebellion against the Council. Amira was flanked by her three sisters of magic, Uzma, Iman, and Mina, born of the same purpose as she. Their presence comforted her as she worried for the fate of her teacher. Qadir had taught her to conjure demons and dark spirits, and she wondered if the Council would persecute her as well.

Uzma felt the worry in Amira's energy field and held her hand, giving it a light squeeze to show her support. Mina and Iman beamed out a protective force field, encapsulating the four of them in light. They thought about how Amira must feel to have her teacher prosecuted before the community.

Qadir was always the most feared of temple priests by the citizens of Ur. His solitary habits cast suspicion on his activities; his dark aura accented by the deep lines on his face repelled most from wanting to be in his presence. Qadir's energy gave him an imposing countenance rather than his physical height, which was just average. Since being assigned to instruct Amira in the dark arts, she was the only one who entered his chamber.

The sanctuary was an underground room dedicated to magic in all its forms. Ritual tools were displayed on shelves around the room, including daggers with blades of all lengths and handles made from pearl, onyx, obsidian, and brass. Wands imbedded with multitudes of gemstones adorned one table, while a large cauldron stood steaming in the center of the room. Smoking herbs and incense of all kinds were kept in a cabinet and used for spellcasting to conjure the desired spirits or to banish them. A large collection of magical spears and swords was securely housed in a locked case that stretched the length of the room. Books were everywhere, on shelves along the walls and strewn on tables, the tops of which were coated in the drippings of large candles, the room's only source of light.

Amira marveled at the secrets held within the chamber, but Qadir limited her lessons to the nature of the dark spirits, not allowing her to touch the magical implements locked in the large case. She was in awe of him, and his cruelty during the lessons was accepted as part of the necessary path to understand the shadowy nature of the spirits she called. A sharp slap of a whip to her leg, when she mispronounced difficult words in a spell, was not uncommon; chaining her to a chair as she read was a regular occurrence. She trusted him to do what was necessary to make her a disciplined student, adept at her craft. Watching the gentle teaching methods of those who instructed Iman, Mina, and Uzma made Amira feel as though the others were soft and incapable of the power she could wield as a result of the pain and torment Qadir included in her lessons. It hardened her over time and made her feel superior to the others.

Mina noticed how Amira flinched at her own mistakes if Qadir was nearby. She was saddened by how he controlled Amira and scarred her lovely, pale skin. Thankful for the kindness of her teacher, Hala, she was always attentive when being instructed about the moon phases and spell correspondences. Mina dreamt of helping others with her knowledge in addition to the special purpose for which they trained. Together, they were the Triad Witches, born to protect the Scrolls of the Four Winds. Mina took pride in her task and drew happiness from the friendship she shared with her sisters. Although each was born of different parents, they felt a bond that rivaled that of any blood relation.

Now as they waited for the verdict, the bond was used to support Amira in her time of need. Of late, Iman, Uzma, and Mina had noticed Amira growing distant, withdrawn from their usual lively interactions, and they were concerned that she was taking on the murky energy exuded by Qadir. Amira stood erect, her muscles tense with fear of losing her teacher. He had taught her to obey him, and she would do as he commanded to please him. Only he had the strength to direct her.

The High Priest presiding over the Council spoke: "Qadir, for your crimes against a fellow priest and against the laws of the Temple, you should be excommunicated from our midst. Because the Watchers have selected you to educate Amira of the Triad Witches in a purpose that is essential to the welfare of all who live on this planet, we decree that you will continue to do so."

Amira let out an audible breath. She had not realized that she stopped breathing when the High Priest began to speak.

"However," the High Priest continued, "you are no longer eligible for an elevation in status within the temple nor within the community at large. Your duties are restricted to obligations dictated by The Watchers. No longer will you walk among the temple priests. No longer will you take meals with us. The exception to your solitude will be interactions with your student. Remove yourself from our presence."

Qadir had not moved during the sentencing; his facial expression did not change. He said nothing as he turned and walked the stretch between onlookers, hands clasped casually behind his back. He did not look to either side. The Witches stood looking down from the balcony as he departed. Amira watched in amazement as his aura clouded over and grew darker than a moonless night. She understood the Council's reluctance to go against The Watchers, yet they worried for Amira under the tutelage of one so evil and headstrong.

Iman hugged Amira to share her joy in retaining her teacher. She knew the bond they shared and felt Amira's relief at his ability to continue her lessons. Iman was optimistic that whatever darkness Qadir exposed Amira to would be countered by her innate goodness and the support of her sisters. She believed that good would always triumph, so Iman focused on spreading light and happiness to all she came in contact with. Hope and faith were her weapons, and the hug she gave Amira was loaded with them.

Amira looked over Iman's shoulder, watching Qadir walk from the room. She would give him some time, and then go to him. Part of her was pleased that she was his only human contact; part was anxious at the mood this would place him in. She pictured her blood running freely as he balanced his temper with the whip against her legs. Amira resolved to make sure her lessons were perfect, the recitation of complex spells performed without error. She would make him proud and forget about his intention to rise to power. She gave Iman an absent smile as she pushed her gently away. She did not take her eyes off the door Qadir exited and followed in the direction of his departure.

The others closed the gap left by Amira's withdrawal, troubled by her strong affiliation to Qadir. They were aware of his abusive tactics and could not understand how a woman as strong and attractive as

Amira could allow such treatment. She certainly did not tolerate it from any other man. If a male in the community even looked at her the wrong way, she unleashed a venomous attack that would make his energy shrivel to nothing. They had seen the results of her power and so had many of the town dwellers. Word had quickly spread among the men to avoid Amira and resist her allure. Qadir held her in some kind of a trance that the others had not been able to break. But they would keep trying.

Amira ran out of the building to catch up with Qadir, her earlier decision to give him some time gone by the wayside. He heard her approach but did not pause or turn to acknowledge her. She ran up to him, panting from the exertion, and adopted his pace as she walked beside him. No words were exchanged for several minutes as Qadir continued his steady pace, hands behind his back. Amira was content to be in his presence and waited for him to be ready to speak.

He stopped and turning to face Amira, backhanded her across the face, the smile that had begun to creep to her lips obliterated in one stroke. The attack knocked her backwards, and she landed hard on her coccyx bone sending waves of nausea and pain up her spine. She looked up at him, tears welling in her eyes, wondering what had prompted him to strike her. His evil glare kept her seated on the ground, fearing to rub her cheek where his hand had made contact with her jaw. Without a word, he walked away.

From the doorway of the temple, the Triad Witches stood aghast at Qadir's assault on Amira. They approached her slowly, giving her time to gather her emotions. Iman and Uzma each took an arm to help her up. She did not look them in the eyes as she thanked them. She brushed herself off, wincing when she grazed the base of her spine.

Iman offered to heal the bruised areas, but the pain was not so much physical as emotional. Her injuries would worsen and become colorful by morning, but for now, she desired only to be alone with her aches. She again left the group behind to follow her teacher. It was a long walk to his chamber, and it would give her time to think of what she had done and how to make it up to him. When she arrived at the door to Qadir's sanctuary, she hesitated before knocking. Her fist was raised to rap on the door, and before she could strike it, he commanded her to enter.

She stood silently before him, the spot where he struck her beginning to swell and bruise.

"I see your loyalty overcomes common sense," he leered.

"My loyalty stands with you," she said, head held high.

"Does it? Now that I am confined to interact only with you, does that give you some sense of superiority over me?"

"Not at all. I feel privileged to be your student and pleased that the relationship is allowed to continue."

"My allegiance is to no one but myself. I do not need you or anyone else in order to wield my power," he said.

"I understand that you stay with me out of obligation on behalf of The Watchers. I would not expect one as powerful as you to take interest in me otherwise."

He eyed her up and down. She felt him embrace her curves with his eyes. It was uncomfortable for her to be viewed in such a way, more so than when he exacted his brutal punishments. Had she not been his student, his interest in her would have taken a much different form.

"You will be of use to me one way or the other."

Amira waited for him to explain, relieved that his plans included her.

"There are other roads to power. Authority bestowed by the High Priest and Council of the temple pales in comparison to that which could be attained from the spirits."

Amira listened, her body erect, ignoring the pain in her face and buttocks.

"I have a plan to obtain the most powerful magical tools in existence," Qadir declared, pointing his forefinger to the sky.

"What can I do to help?"

"You will be the primary ingredient in acquiring what I seek."

"What tools do you seek, Qadir?" asked Amira, intrigued by his enthusiasm.

"The Scrolls of the Four Winds."

⚡ 1 ⚡

New Hope, Pennsylvania, present day

The waxing moon was halfway to full. Victoria Perry had chosen New Hope for its quaint feel, artistic bent, and large pagan community. She was also drawn to this historic town in Pennsylvania because she sensed the presence of Iman, Mina, and Uzma, her ancient sisters. Together with Victoria, they were the Triad Witches, united in a common purpose. Their energetic imprint was unmistakable.

The vacant storefront on Main Street was central to sidewalk traffic; increasing the likelihood that they would find their way into her antique shop. While she would have preferred a building with a more Victorian feel, the colonial was spacious and perfect for her purposes. It had an adequate area to display antiques, a separate room in the back for meetings, and a basement for storage. An apartment upstairs allowed her to live above and work below. *As above so below*, she thought.

Her realtor, George Washburn, had been too friendly in his manner. He did not notice when Victoria bristled as he threw out one personal question after another. She did not like to reveal information about herself and resented his barrage of questions about where she came from, her last business, her age—of all things, the standard don't-ask-that-of-a-woman question. She was vague in her responses, as she answered—Italy, unique clothing, and "Now, Mr. Washburn, a lady doesn't reveal her age!" If she had told him the truth, he would not have believed her.

She could have told him her age in this lifetime, but it was best to act coy. She was only 35 this time around, and had spent most of those years coming back into her power and locating the others. As for her business in Benevento, in her last lifetime, she catered to the Strega, the local covens of Italian Witches, selling ritual supplies and clothing. Witches had occupied Benevento for several thousand years. A massive walnut tree was the gathering place of witches who worshipped the goddess Diana. When the Duke of Benevento converted to Christianity in 662 A.D., he had their sacred tree cut down. Her customers remained steadfast in their beliefs despite their oppressive history and regularly practiced their craft, necessitating the replenishing of candles, herbs, and incense. Victoria looked back upon that time as one of profit and camaraderie. The witches of Benevento had treated her as one of their own. She had not felt a sense of belonging since being a part of the Triad Witches.

Victoria thanked the realtor, and the stars, as he handed her the keys at the settlement table. His insincere sales approach grated on her nerves. It was strenuous to hold her tongue and her power at bay as he rambled on and on. The transaction had ended on its own before she chose to put an end to it herself. She was glad to be rid of him and looked forward to setting up shop.

The boxes arrived that afternoon on time, as did the installer from the sign company. Over the centuries, Victoria had found that the moon in Sagittarius was a good time for completing chores. She directed the movers in placing her personal items upstairs and her wares downstairs. A daunting task was before her to get settled in her personal space, while creating an environment to ensnare her targets. Their energetic attachment to historic objects Victoria had saved from the distant past would lure them. There was much to do, and it was time to begin recruiting her team.

With the movers gone, Victoria stood in the center of what would be her meeting room, closed her eyes, and lifted her arms just below shoulder height, elbows bent with her palms up. Her feet were planted firmly on the floor, shoulder width apart. Qadir had taught her this stance to open communication with the spirits. Thoughts of him flashed through her mind. She looked around the room to ensure he had not joined her unexpectedly. Qadir had a way of lurking in the shadows, watching her without her knowledge. Sudden thoughts of him warned her of his presence. Satisfied that she was alone, she began her ritual. With a raised voice, she thanked the spirits for their assistance in acquiring the building and requested help in finding the appropriate members of her new group. A phantom breeze brushed through Victoria's long black hair and she smiled, knowing she had been heard.

Communicating with the spirits always made her hungry, so she set out to explore the local cuisine. New Hope had abundant culinary options, everything from casual fare to elegant dining. Victoria followed her intuition as she walked down Main Street. People strolled along the sidewalks. The unusual was commonplace in this town, so those she passed did not react to her appearance—statuesque with long, flowing black hair, large, dark eyes, and high cheekbones, her body layered in black fabric that was form-fitting underneath and sheer and flowing on top. The tourists were dressed mostly in denim jeans and casual tops, but were accustomed to shop owners dressing in noteworthy outfits. Victoria fit right in.

Her internal radar called her to make a right onto Mechanic Street. A restaurant called *Esca* caught her eye and drew her to its door. She sensed that more than a good meal awaited her in this charming establishment. White clothed tables sat amidst the golden glow of the walls, punctuated with tiny light fixtures and dark wood chairs.

The hostess seated Victoria at a small table against the North wall and handed her a menu. *I always land in my direction of power*, she mused. Victoria's strong alignment with the North amplified her influence. The magical correspondences of this compass direction bestowed additional force to her already impressive powers. She recalled her ancient lessons taught by Qadir. He had emphasized midnight as her time of greatest power and that she was aligned with the element of Earth. She learned the deep esoteric meanings of these correspondences over time with Qadir's help.

Victoria watched the waiter approach her table. He was handsome and well-built, with dark hair and striking blue eyes. The tight black T-shirt fit snugly around his muscular arms and emphasized his slim waist. The strong jaw line and five o'clock shadow gave him casual good looks. His broad smile showed off his straight white teeth framed with generous lips. Victoria found herself slightly aroused as she noticed he was checking her out as well.

"My name is Ethan, and I'll be attending to your every need this evening." He paused and smiled, emphasizing the double entendre. "May I start you off with a beverage?" His eyes went from her cleavage to the ring finger of her left hand. He always made sure his conquests were single. No wedding band gave him the signal to plow ahead.

Victoria watched Ethan as he spoke. She opened herself to his auric field, taking in his energy to receive a vast store of knowledge about his nature. She was flooded with images of Ethan charming solitary female diners for large tips or a sexual rendezvous. His self-absorbed, over-confident nature was the perfect combination. Victoria found it easy to manipulate this type of male. Playing to his inflated ego would allow her to mold him any way she chose.

She smiled fetchingly at him. "A glass of Cabernet, please."

Ethan returned her look with his standard come-hither gaze, forged with the experience of dozens of similar encounters. He knew this woman wanted him. The view of her cleavage was a deciding factor in giving her the opportunity to indulge in his sexual prowess. "*Coming right up,*" he teased.

Ethan returned with her drink, making an exaggerated bow as he placed the glass of Cabernet in front of her. She held his gaze as he straightened.

"What can I get for such a beautiful lady?" he inquired, taking a pen from behind his ear and opening his order pad.

So full of himself, Victoria thought. "Whatever you recommend, Ethan," she said, watching his ego expand before her eyes.

He liked the way she willingly gave herself over to him, even as she ordered. "I'll be back with a surprise just for you."

You're the one who will be surprised, Victoria smiled at her plan. Ethan thought the smile was meant for him. Grasping the wine glass, Victoria read the energetic imprint left by Ethan. She saw her ample breasts from Ethan's perspective and sensed his anticipation of an exceptionally rewarding evening with her. Through the vibrations on the glass, she saw his hand on her breast and her full lips drawn to his. She admitted to herself that the scene was stimulating; he was very good at tantalizing his sexual partners. The superficiality of his intentions did not surprise her. Victoria took a deep breath to clear the image from her mind. With that out of the way, she was able to see deeper into his nature. She saw his need to be accepted; his use of charisma to obtain sexual satisfaction, and his ultimate rejection of the women who hoped that wild sex would develop into a committed relationship. Ethan's relationships were bereft of intimacy. He feared revealing his superficiality and lack of understanding. He was drawn to affairs where he could derive a benefit, then release the person before having to reciprocate.

Her visions were disrupted by Ethan's return. He proudly placed the plate in front of her. "Insalata Caprese: slices of Italian plum tomatoes topped with fresh mozzarella cheese and basil, dressed with virgin olive oil for the lady. Please enjoy this while waiting for your entrée. Is there *anything* else I can do for you?" Ethan was portraying the formal waiter/gigolo role. The use of another double entendre was not lost on Victoria.

She played along, "Nothing that would be appropriate in this setting." She took a sip of wine; then slowly ran her tongue across her upper lip, keeping eye contact until his eyes drifted to her cleavage again.

Ethan got it, and pictured himself getting it, maybe as soon as tonight. He gave an acknowledging smile and gave a short bow before waiting on the next table. Victoria rolled her eyes. *Men are all the same*, she thought.

Ethan returned with her entrée. "Polpette di Granchio," he said with rehearsed pronunciation. "Sautéed crab cakes drizzled with an orange basil aioli. It's my personal favorite. If its succulence pleases you, maybe you'll consider having a drink with me when my shift ends this evening."

"If I agree to a drink, will you introduce me to other things that might please me?"

"I am at your service, ready to satisfy your needs," he whole-heartedly promised. Ethan always delivered sexual satisfaction to his partners, at least as far as he knew.

Finished with her meal, she motioned to Ethan with a slow curl of her forefinger. He immediately responded. "Dinner was exceptional, Ethan." She told him he had made wonderful choices for her meal. "How about meeting me at my place when you get off work? Bring a bottle of wine with you to help me christen my new place. It's on Main Street, second floor of 'Victoria's Antiques'. That's my store, and I live above it. The entrance is on the side. Everything is still in boxes. Maybe you can help me unpack."

"It will be my pleasure, Victoria," he took her hand and kissed it gently on the back, letting his lips linger to give her a preview of the evening's activities.

How cliché, Victoria judged amidst the startling realization that his lips on her skin made her tingle. Maybe the wine had gotten the best of her. *Only do what is necessary to accomplish the goal*, she chided herself.

*   *   *

Ethan pranced up the walkway, bottle of Cabernet in hand. He had grabbed a bottle from the restaurant. It was the same type as Victoria was drinking at dinner. She had seemed to like it, so he figured he would stick with a sure thing. He pictured Victoria waiting for him at the door, wearing a revealing frock that would set the tone for the rest of the evening. His energy was high, even though the hour was late, 11 pm; his job had acclimated him to a late-night schedule. Ethan's knock beckoned Victoria, who answered the door wearing the same outfit she had had on at the restaurant. He found her intriguing, and the tight black top and slacks accentuated every curve and shrouded her in mystery.

He stepped through the doorway, displaying the wine bottle, label-side up, cradled over his left forearm. He picked up this action at the restaurant when showing patrons special bottles of wine to emphasize the quality, and it quickly became habit. Having walked over in the dark, his eyes were already adjusted to the dim light inside her apartment. Candlelight flickered around the room, creating shadows and soft illumination that added to Victoria's intensity. Darkness was her preference. She could manipulate the energies much better in the absence of light. Her pupils were dilated, taking advantage of her cat-like ability to see in the dark. For Victoria, it was as good as daylight in the diffuse lighting. Over the centuries, she performed the bulk of her work at midnight, and so functioned comfortably in poorly lit environments.

The boxes were arranged along the walls and silhouetted by small flames. Furniture was in place: a couch, coffee table, end tables, and chair-and-a-half with thick cushions and an ottoman. Ethan knew it looked like a good spot to make love. Victoria invited him to have a seat. He chose the sofa, figuring he could coax her onto the big chair later. Ethan could not take his eyes off of her as she gracefully crossed the room and bent over to retrieve the wine glasses out of a box marked "fragile" and the corkscrew from a box with "kitchen" written on the side. The back of her was as tantalizing as the front. He anticipated an incredible experience with her. She poured them each a healthy serving of the red nectar.

"I'm looking forward to seeing the place when you're done with it," Ethan subtly invited himself back. *That's odd*, he thought, *I don't usually anticipate a return visit with a one-night stand.* He mentally reviewed his last few conquests. They had achieved much higher ratings before he met Victoria. It was like comparing chicken fingers to filet mignon, and he much preferred eating the latter. She had an air of sophistication that was slightly intimidating, but he overcame his feeling of inadequacy by reminding himself how impressed she would be when he finally had the chance to pleasure her.

"I believe this will be more than a one-night stand for you, Ethan," Victoria casually stated.

"What? I, well, uh, what do you mean?" Ethan felt the scene of sexual perfection slip from his mind, replaced with wonderment at how she knew what he was thinking. His face warmed and flushed at getting caught in his planning. For the first time in years, he was uncertain how to approach this incredibly unusual woman. It was too late to play innocent.

"Just what I said. Tonight will be the beginning of a new life for you, if you choose to go down the path with me."

"Hey, wait a minute. Don't think I'm going to marry you any time soon!" Ethan put the glass down and started to get up from the couch.

"Relax," she commanded, as she put her hand on his shoulder, releasing a calming energy into him. He immediately sat down. "Don't flatter yourself. Marriage to you or anyone else is the last thing I'm interested in."

"Then what *do* you want?"

"I want to teach you things you never dreamed of learning."

"I can't imagine you can show me anything I haven't already tried in the way of sex, but I'm willing to let you have at it," Ethan said, his confidence returning.

"So single-minded and shallow. Maybe I chose the wrong person. I thought you were ready," Victoria shook her head in mock disappointment.

"Wait, chose me for what? Ready for what?"

"I'm afraid it has nothing to do with sex, so you're probably not going to be interested," she taunted him.

"The depth of my interest will depend on how it compares to sex. You have me all worked up, and it's hard to switch gears. No pun intended"

"I can take care of that," she said, touching her middle and forefingers to the center of his forehead. He took a deep breath as she soothed his sexual appetite. It was only temporary, but this was important and she needed to have his full attention. Victoria could see he was now putting his hormones away and opening to a broader range of possibilities.

"In the restaurant, I was looking for a man with a strong sense of self who could act as my second-in-command. I'm recruiting for a highly specialized group of people to develop their natural gifts. You are the first to be contacted."

"I'm listening." Ethan was ready to cooperate.

Victoria looked at the clock. It was 11:45 pm, only 15 minutes before the Witching Hour. "Our group will form the coven, a coven of Witches." She took a sip of wine.

"And you want me to do what? Be the human sacrifice?" Ethan was suspicious. He knew there was something different about her, something mysterious. *She was a witch, for god sakes.*

"Of course not. Witches don't sacrifice people, or animals for that matter. That is just negative press to turn people against us. I want you to be the sole male energy in the group. The rest will be women."

"So it is about sex!" Ethan grinned, half kidding, half hoping. Victoria had only wiped away his immediate sexual urge, not his overall tendency toward the desire.

"There may be times when we need that type of ritual performed, yes, but it goes far beyond that. We will be doing important work together, you and I, with support from the group. If you wish to become part of this, I need your word that you will be loyal to me and keep the secrets that I share with you," Victoria said, knowing that his loyalty extended only to himself.

"So what's in it for me?" Ethan inquired. He knew several women in the area that were practicing witches, so he was not a stranger to the concept; but he had never considered it as an option for himself. In the way of religious understanding, he had only a forced Presbyterian Church experience from childhood. It was a time to daydream and think of what he would do after the service had ended.

"What is your desire?" Victoria said, her voice like liquid velvet washing over Ethan. She looked at the antique clock on the fireplace mantle. It was 11:55 pm. The escapement clicked as the spring loaded, readying the chime.

"I submitted a resume for a director of marketing position at Sandlock Corporation, but they haven't called me. Even if it's not *the* director position, I'd like to have a high-paying job there."

"It shall be done. We will concentrate on that as our first lesson in spellcasting."

"Okay, I'll give it a try," Ethan said with a shrug.

"No! This is not something you enter into lightly. It is a way of life, a total immersion, calling for devotion to The Craft and to me. And total loyalty to me. You will never be the same. Decide!" said Victoria, the smoothness in her voice replaced by a booming command.

Startled, Ethan's mind reeled. He could feel Victoria's power and wanted to become potent in his own right. There would be no stopping him once he learned all she had to teach him. "I'll do it. I accept," Ethan said decisively. The first stroke sounded, "Bong!"

It was midnight. Victoria lifted a portable-sized cast iron cauldron five inches in diameter from behind a chair and put it on the coffee table. It was filled with strange-smelling leaves. She pulled a dagger from a sheath hanging around her waist. "Bong!" Ethan wondered how he had missed it before and nervously drank some wine to steady himself. Pointing the dagger northeast, Victoria spoke, "I cast this circle to protect us from all harm, and to contain all energy conjured therein."

"Bong!"

She took a lighter with a long neck and touched the flame to the contents of the cauldron. Thick billows of sweet and bitter fragrance floated out of the vessel.

"Bong!"

Victoria chanted, "On this night of the waxing moon, I call all spirits into the room, to greet a newly chosen student, who needs help at being prudent."

"Bong!"

"Guide him with all your might so that his potential will take flight."

"Bong!"

A gust of wind came from within the room, blowing her long black hair across her face.

"Bong!"

She turned to Ethan. "Stand up and repeat after me. I hereby dedicate my body and soul to the study of The Craft, to my High Priestess, Victoria, and to the gods and goddesses."

"Bong!"

Ethan stood, watching the invisible forces blow through Victoria's hair and spread the smoke rising from the cauldron. He repeated the words.

"Bong!"

He was feeling lightheaded from the wine and the smoke billowing from the cauldron. Victoria took over the ritual, "I bestow upon you, Ethan Talbot, the Craft name of Khalil, which means 'friend.' You have entered into the circle as a friend."

"Bong!"

The room became slightly darker, and Ethan felt a weight descend onto him as though entering through the tip of his head. It seemed to melt into his body and become part of him, spreading heat from his core to his extremities. A bright flash of light filled his mind, and then gradually dissipated, leaving him with a floating sensation. A sense of fulfillment enveloped him. She had bewitched him.

"Bong!"

Through the fog of his thoughts, Ethan wondered how she knew his last name. "Khalil," he repeated dreamily as the last chime gave way to silence.

"Oh great spirits, Khalil desires a job at Sandlock Corporation. Bestow the right position for him as a reward for his loyalty to us. Khalil, as an employee of Sandlock, you will work to accomplish my goals first, your company's second."

Ethan nodded in agreement. He was a rebel by nature, yet to go against Victoria would be a monumental mistake. She commanded forces that were beyond his understanding. His role at this time was to cater to her will. Later he would find a way to harness this power for his own purposes.

"To go against me, Khalil, is the equivalent of treason, and will be dealt with as such," Victoria stated. Ethan knew it was not a threat, for she said it with calm conviction. He thought it a strange coincidence that she kept responding to his thoughts.

Victoria drew the dagger, pointing it again northeast. "I remove this circle and close the gate. I banish all spirits and extend my gratitude for your assistance during this dedication ceremony. Blessed be." The circle was complete.

Ethan was also released and sat down heavily on the couch. He gulped his wine. "I'll get us a little snack to stabilize us. It's always a good idea to eat something small after a ritual." She went into the kitchen and returned with an assortment of mini pastries. Ethan chose one at random and popped it in his mouth. He had been plunged into a daze he was finding hard to shake.

"You had an energetic shift during the ritual, so you'll feel a bit off-balance until tomorrow morning. Best to go home and get a good night's sleep."

Ethan was going to be an interesting case. Once he shook off the initial shock to his system, he would be a good student. The way he absorbed the energy so easily made her optimistic about his potential. She was confident that getting the job would convince Ethan that his loyalty would get him all that he desires. She would show him what real power tasted like.

Ethan nodded to Victoria as his eyes grazed her cleavage one last time, his lust now competing with the sensation of the newfound power. He stood slowly, almost staggering, and trudged out of the apartment still in a trance. Victoria watched as he closed the door gently behind him.

* * *

It was noon before Ethan's eyes fluttered open in response to the bright sunlight peeking through the heavy drapes in his bedroom. He lay diagonally along the queen-sized bed, sheets and blankets bunched up in complete disarray. He threw his arm across his eyes. He didn't have to be at work until four o'clock this afternoon, so could take some time to acclimate to the day. The taste of wine still lay on his tongue. That had been some potent stuff. Sleep had reduced the dense fog that had lain across his mind the night before to a light mist.

Images of Victoria's dimly lit apartment, her beauty in the candlelight, and the eerie ritual she performed flooded his mind. It was rare that he was invited to a woman's home and not allowed to show her his expertise in the bedroom. What had he promised her? Did his loyalty to her mean that he was not allowed to sleep with other women? It did not seem as though she intended to enter into a physically intimate relationship with him.

The strangeness of the evening was punctuated by the odd smell of the smoke coming from the cauldron and the phantom breeze that blew around Victoria. Had he been hallucinating? The wine seemed untainted. He had brought the bottle, so it could not have been drugged. Victoria could have put something in the glasses. She requested that he bring wine and had time to coat the glasses. She took them out of a box, but that could have been a ploy to throw him off. Even so, he suspected that it was not the wine that had intoxicated him. Whenever he was near her, he felt lightheaded. It had happened in the restaurant as well.

Ethan was severely handicapped in understanding what had transpired last evening. There were other forces present during the ritual. Victoria had called them spirits; but what kind of spirits, he could only guess. He had entered unfamiliar territory and was taken off balance by the experience. He tried to wrap his mind around the incident, but found it exceedingly difficult, having nothing to compare it to. This was a most unique occurrence. Never having dabbled in the realm of the occult, Ethan was struggling in his ability to contemplate what had transpired last evening. All he had to go on were his basic observations and the sensations that he experienced during the rite.

The heaviness that seemed to wriggle inside of him was the most disconcerting of all. He had absorbed some sort of entity, a dark energy that he saw enter the room, then disappear into his body. He did not feel possessed, at least not the way possession was depicted in horror films. There was a density to him that he had never felt before, a solidity that made him feel more aware and less vulnerable.

Ethan decided to get up and test the new strength he felt. His usual start-of-the-day routine commenced without incident. Dressing for work in his uniform black pants and black shirt, he gazed at himself in the mirror. He spent several minutes each day admiring himself and practicing facial expressions to entice the ladies. He saw something different as he peered out from behind the face he knew so well. There was a sparkle in his eyes that had been absent until now. They seemed to have a similar intensity as he saw in Victoria's eyes. A smile crept across his lips. The first glimmer of power was showing itself. "Khalil," she had whispered, bestowing upon him his power name, the name of initiation, and introducing him to a new phase of his life.

Ethan enjoyed his newfound energy. His feet planted firmly on the ground with a heaviness and fortitude that defied challenge. He knew he had embarked on a new path, as Victoria had said he would. Astonishing to think that he had hesitated. What he needed was knowledge about this new world. Victoria would teach him some things, like how to use his powers to get anything he wished for, like money, women, and a life of ample playtime. He had no idea what he was capable of. He fantasized about reading the minds of women he desired and putting them into a trance to succumb to his whim. Victoria knew the extent of his new abilities, but he had to be careful with her. She enticed and spooked him at the same time, and he did not want to make her angry. Some of his learning would need to come from books. This was not his preferred means of getting information, but it would have to do until Victoria decided to open up about what she did to him. He still had suspicions about Victoria's motives and did not trust that her teachings would be objective. Ethan wanted a source that had no allegiance whatsoever. Maybe the Internet would serve him better.

He sat at his desk and booted up his computer. His home page was set to Google. He typed "witchcraft" into the search window and was shocked to get 9,500,000 results. Websites that focused on divination using Tarot or astrology, sites that explained the religion of Wicca, spells promising results, witchcraft supplies, the list went on and on. He did not know where to begin. He changed his strategy and went to Amazon.com and typed "witchcraft" into the book search window. It returned over 36,000 results. The first couple entries looked like they might have what he needed. "A Witches' Bible: The Complete Witches Handbook" by Janet Farrar and Stewart Farrar and "Buckland's Complete Book of Witchcraft" by Raymond Buckland. He bought both. He had to start somewhere.

With a couple of hours at his disposal, he decided to stop in and check on Victoria's progress. Victoria's apartment was loaded with boxes, but nothing compared to the number of crates that had been dumped into her storefront. She could use a hand. At the same time, he could pump her for information. His suspicions relating to others always came back to his own nature. His intentions were rarely philanthropic. There was always something in it for himself.

The walk over gave him an opportunity to see the world with his new eyes. Plants, people, and objects seemed to have a glow around them, some had colors of red, blue, or green, and others were simply white. He rubbed his eyes a few times, thinking it was glare from a reflection or a stray eyelash creating strange visual effects. Maybe it was the mist that surrounded his mind since waking. Ethan turned the corner and saw the sign for "Victoria's Antiques." A bell rang to announce his entrance.

Victoria's head popped up from behind a pile of boxes, her legs ankle-deep in packing materials. The floor looked like a barnyard filled with synthetic hay. Urns, statues, glassware, and furniture had been unpacked but not set up for display. She looked great in her snug T-shirt and form-fitting jeans. The strange visions left his mind as he focused on her physique.

"Hey, pretty lady. Thought I'd stop in and see if I could lend a hand," Ethan said.

"I could certainly use one. Two would be better. Are you feeling up to it after last night?" she asked, knowing that he was more capable today than he had been before she enhanced him.

"I feel fantastic," Ethan said enthusiastically. "Must have been the wine. We should get another bottle."

Victoria let it go. "Glad to hear that you've embraced the new energy. Not everyone is capable of handling the shift." In fact, she had seen some initiates react with utter despair, ending in self-destruction. Their weakness was a casualty that could not be avoided. It was the chance she had to take to build her legion. Most lasted only months before needing to be replaced, their stamina inadequate to withstand the energy that was introduced into their feeble vessels. The willingness that the majority of people had to hand over their personal power to someone else was the blessing and the curse of Victoria's efforts. She insisted on their total loyalty and willingness to do her bidding, yet required determination that extended beyond her control. It was a delicate balance, one that was needed in order to achieve the potential of the adept. Yes, balance was important to manage many things, especially the equilibrium necessary to wield her ancient artifacts.

"I'm capable of handling anything you throw at me," Ethan bragged, hoping she would decide to start his lessons early. Victoria smiled at Ethan's bravado. His ego made it so easy to influence him.

"Let's start by getting the empty boxes and packing into the dumpster." They flattened boxes and carried armfuls of shredded paper and Styrofoam peanuts out the back door and threw them into the dumpster. With the clutter removed, it was easier to see how much progress had been made. All of the items she had intended for sale were in this room. Others had been stowed away in the basement, not meant for prying eyes or curious hands. These objects carried with them occult significance beyond the abilities of the average practitioner to control. She, herself, even with her vast knowledge, extensive training, and centuries of practice, struggled with one grouping of items in particular.

"You have quite an inventory," Ethan commented. His eyes wandered around the room, touching each item he found appealing. "How much is this one?" he asked, holding up an urn the color of oxblood with a crackle-finish and brass scrollwork at the base.

"Two hundred seventy five dollars," Victoria responded without looking directly at Ethan or the urn. She could see it through his eyes. She could feel the desire within him to own beautiful things.

"Wow," he set it carefully back down on the table.

Victoria looked around and was pleased that she could see the floor. "You've been a tremendous help. I couldn't have done it so quickly without you."

"Khalil, at your service, High Priestess," he smiled and bowed. It felt natural for him to behave this way toward her. He wanted to impress her and please her in ways other than sexual. The attraction he felt to her body was nothing compared to the way her energy drew him to her, making him want to be around her, to do things for her. He was sorry that work had to disrupt service to his high priestess. "I'd like to stay and help you finish, but it's time for me to go serve my other master at the restaurant."

"I understand. While you're there, keep your eyes open for anyone you think would be a good addition to the coven. Feel the energy of people you wait on. Look for a solid auric field," she instructed.

"What is an auric field?" inquired Ethan.

"Your first lesson. An auric field is the energy that surrounds the human body and all living things, for that matter. Each entity has a different energetic signature, marked by its emotional state, physical health, and spiritual beliefs. Distinguish those who are appropriate for our group by determining if the energy is smooth and complete around the body as opposed to energy that has holes in it and feels jagged. You were seeing them around objects on your way over here."

"I did see something on the way over, but wasn't sure what to make of it." He was growing used to her knowing things he had not told her. "I've never noticed anything like that before. Will I be able to control it or will it just happen?" Ethan wondered.

"You had a shift. You will be aware of energies that have been around you always, yet were undetectable until now. You have been awakened."

"This is going to be interesting. I'll stop by tomorrow before work and let you know how I made out. If there's anything else I can help with, just leave it until tomorrow." He left the shop through the front door, the tinkle of the bell announcing his departure.

⚡ 2 ⚡

The bell was decades old and had an antique patina that showed its age. The clang it made when the door hit the lip let Victoria know a customer had entered the store. She peeked out from the doorway of the backroom and spied a girl in her late twenties moving cautiously into the store. The drab green jacket over a dingy white T-shirt and brown corduroys made her unruly hair look almost neat in comparison. The absence of cosmetics made her features practically disappear into her rosy complexion. Her shoulders were slightly raised in a shrug and her head was pulled down toward her chest. Over the years, she had tried less and less to make herself look presentable. It never mattered anyway. No one was interested in getting to know her, regardless of what she looked like. Victoria had a remedy for what ailed her. She watched her for a few more seconds, and then came further into the showroom.

"Greetings, my dear," said Victoria. "Welcome to my shop."

"You have beautiful things here," she replied. "I'm being careful not to break anything."

"Nonsense, you look as graceful as a gazelle. I'm sure you'll be just fine. Take your time and look around," Victoria invited.

"Thank you," she said, her head lifting to full height. The shoulders remained in their heightened state.

"My name is Victoria. And you are?"

"Heather. Heather Moorcroft."

"Nice to meet you, Heather. Feel free to browse as long as you like. I'm still working to unpack these ancient beauties, so if you don't find anything today, please be sure to stop back and see what I have hiding in these boxes."

"Thank you," said Heather, now lowering her shoulders. She turned away from Victoria and started to systematically check each item, making sure not to miss anything. Her eyes touched so many wonderful statues, vases, and chairs. She wished she had the money to decorate her apartment with them.

Victoria removed packing material from boxes with her back to Heather. She did not want to spook the poor child prematurely. This was a fragile soul she was dealing with. Victoria sent out her energy to pull information from Heather. The touch of it made Heather look behind her feeling as though she was being watched, only to find Victoria busy unpacking boxes. She shrugged it off and continued shopping. Victoria liked that Heather was sensitive to energy. She was wide open and vulnerable. No wonder she acted like she could be attacked at any moment. Her essence was continuously leaking from her auric field.

Heather caught sight of a bronze statue of a figure dancing in the middle of a circle. She picked it up and looked more closely, now seeing that the figure had multiple arms and a headdress. The circle had small flames protruding around the perimeter.

"Shiva, the Universal Godhead," said Victoria.

Heather looked up, then back at the statue. "There's something about it that draws me."

"It's a powerful piece, perfect for your personal altar."

"I don't have an altar," said Heather apologetically, feeling once again that she had missed out on something important.

"Never too late to create one," encouraged Victoria. "Shiva is the destroyer of evil in the Hindu religion, but has other aspects as well. He is the supreme god of Hinduism capable of creation as well as destruction. He preserves, and blesses. He pardons sins and is all-powerful."

"Wow, that's a good spirit to have on your side! And I can certainly use all the help I can get," admitted Heather.

"Help with what, my dear?" Victoria put her hand on Heather's shoulder. Heather felt heat penetrate through her shirt, past her skin and muscles, and deep into her bones. Victoria watched Heather's eyes brighten and her posture straighten in response to her touch.

"It's a long story. You don't want to hear it."

"How about I make some tea and we can sit in the window seat while you tell me your story. It may help to talk about it," Victoria soothed Heather.

"I don't usually get offers like this, so I'll take you up on it, if you're sure it's not too much trouble," Heather said, trying to hold back her relief at having someone to talk to. Being surrounded by beautiful things and an accepting person was giving her a tremendous boost. The sudden burst of energy made her want to tell Victoria everything.

"I'll make the tea, you make yourself comfortable."

Victoria walked toward the kitchenette she had set up in the backroom. Heather watched her, grateful for Victoria's attention. She was the closest thing to a friend Heather had had in years. The sun streamed into the large front window bathing the shop in light, yet Victoria walked in shadow as she made her way to the rear of the showroom. The effect struck Heather as odd only for a moment, as she turned her attention to the outside of her newfound haven and watched the traffic of cars and people go by. She felt no attachment to anyone or anything, yet remained hopeful that one day she could have a friend and feel that she belonged. She wondered why Victoria encouraged her to stay. Most people were anxious for her to be on her way.

Victoria returned with two steaming mugs of jasmine green tea. The aroma was soothing, but not as much as Victoria's acceptance and welcoming countenance. Heather wanted to tell Victoria her woes, but did not want to scare her off. If she presented herself as a bother, that would be the end of their friendship. She put down the statue of Shiva and gratefully accepted the hot beverage.

"Tell me everything, from the beginning, and don't worry about my reaction. Everyone has issues of one type or another. Very little would surprise or upset me," Victoria reassured Heather.

Heather was surprised at Victoria's statement. Had she had voiced her concerns without realizing it? Victoria was so tuned into her, it took her off guard. People were not usually this interested.

"Okay, if you insist." Heather pressed her palms against the sides of the mug, trying to warm her hands. Her hands always felt cold when she was nervous.

"My problems go back to childhood. When I was a little kid, my mother could only tolerate my presence for short periods of time before becoming very irritable and tired. I was frequently handed off to whichever family member was closest so that my mother could 'take a break' from me. As I watched my mother walk away, it felt as though my body drained of all life and was replaced by sadness. It felt like it was raining inside of me. The pain of rejection was too much to bear at times. As I grew older, my mother spent less and less time around me, always complaining that she was too tired. I found my mother's sentiment echoed among classmates and neighborhood children. I would not get picked for teams during intramurals; no birthday party invitations came to my house. My existence was and continues to be exceedingly lonely." Heather stared at the steam rising from the mug of tea. She was back in her childhood, feeling the pain that followed her into adulthood.

"All I ever wanted was love and affection. My dream was to be liked and accepted. To be part of a group would be to have a protective shield around me. I felt alienated in most social settings. At parties, I'd sit on a sofa, hoping that someone would speak to me. Do you know what it's like to be alone in a room full of people? The occasional party guest would sit on the couch to munch from the snack bowl on the cocktail table, but would become extremely tired after only a few minutes. Eventually, the person would always move on, thinking that sitting for too long had prompted their fatigue." Her hand shook as she brought the mug to her lips and took a sip of tea.

"I feel better when I'm around people – more energetic. I also feel worse, since, inevitably, I'll be rejected. No one likes to be around me," Heather concluded.

"My dear, do you realize that you have a special gift?"

"What do you mean?"

"You are a psychic vampire, an energy sanguinarian. People feel tired around you, because you feed off the energy of others. Psi-vamps are practically incapable of restoring their energy by other means and insatiable when exposed to large groups of people. Since you are not in a position to be around people too often, when you are, you gulp their essence, hungry to feel the core of their being within you. The draining effect you have on others is why most people avoid you, Heather." *And the primary reason I want you in my coven.*

"Why don't you feel tired around me?"

"I have a very strong auric field around me. That is the energy field all humans have. Mine is impervious to psychic attack; therefore, you are unable to feed off my energy."

"I had no idea that I was taking energy from those around me; I just knew that I felt better when I was around people. I thought that was because I was so lonely. "

"I can teach you how to properly feed and how to control how much energy you pull. Strong individuals are the best to take from and the weak, old, ill, or young are to be avoided. To absorb the energy of an infirm person is to take that illness into you and experience the misery the sickness produces. Over time, you will learn the best ways to pull energy from others in small amounts, trying to limit yourself to several minutes with each person. That way, the subject will not feel drained or repelled by you. Parties are a good place to feed, but not from the couch. Go to where people are moving around. The attendees expend so much energy dancing and drinking, that they are less likely to associate their weariness with a proximity to you," instructed Victoria. She took a sip of her tea.

"Can you teach me? Will you help me?" begged Heather.

"Of course, my dear. I'm having a dinner party. I'd like you to come to my home above the shop, on Wednesday night. I'm having a few other people over that I'd like you to meet. Maybe you'll consider joining our group."

"Are you serious? I've never been invited to anything before. I'd love to come!" Heather's joy was difficult to contain.

"Dinner will be served around 7 pm. Bring yourself and your favorite dessert. Whenever you're invited to a place, always bring an offering of some kind to the hostess. By giving to others, you create abundance in your life. It allows the flow of energy in the universe to be maintained through constant exchange. It is a Universal Law. Be aware of how you choose to maintain the flow or hinder it. You give to others, and you receive abundance in return. To simply take without giving back inhibits your ability to receive."

Heather finished the last drop of tea. "I will! I'll see you on Wednesday! Thank you ever so much," she hugged Victoria. A tingling sensation went through her as when her foot falls asleep and begins to awaken, slightly painful, but somehow pleasant at the same time. "I'd like to buy this statue. It makes me feel as though anything is possible. It will be the first thing I put on my new altar," said Heather, eager to show Victoria that she had been listening.

Victoria waved farewell with a smile. She knew she would reel in the right recruit when she charged the brass image of Shiva with the attraction spell.

* * *

Heather felt renewed by her encounter with Victoria. She had a new friend, a new outlook on life. There was something unusual about Victoria that she could not quite determine. Just the fact that she was willing to spend time with Heather was strange enough, but the sensations that Heather felt each time she and Victoria touched were odd. With a normal person, Heather felt nothing when touched; yet Victoria sent waves of heat and sparks through her. This woman was powerful. Heather wondered if she should be afraid. Nothing that her new friend did was cause to fear. She was kind and was a wonderful listener. What was this unease she felt?

Walking always helped to clear her head. She looked in store windows and at the people passing her by. As her gaze wandered, her eyes fell on a sign she had never noticed before: Psychic Readings by Cassandra. The hand-carved wood sign hung from a wrought iron, scrolled arm over the door. Stars were interspersed among the letters.

Maybe Cassandra could help her understand what she was feeling about this situation There was conflict between wanting to trust Victoria, being uncertain about trusting her own instincts, and not caring, only wanting to develop this new friendship.

Heather mounted the steps and slowly pushed open the door. Her first step into the parlor felt as though she had entered another dimension. The smell of incense and the wax of burning candles welcomed her into the space. Tapestries of ornamental trees and natural settings hung from the walls, capturing and deepening the fragrance. A large crystal ball was clutched in a dragon's claw on the center of the table that stood in front of an overstuffed sofa. The ceiling was high and layered with draped, shimmering fabric of blue and purple.

"Welcome," Cassandra said from the doorway into the reading room.

"Thank you," said Heather. "Do I need to make an appointment for a reading or do you accept walk-ins?"

"This time slot is open in an otherwise full schedule. It was meant for you. Please come in," Cassandra stood aside and beckoned Heather into the reading room.

A round table with several decks of Tarot cards sat in the middle of the room. Incense burned in the corner, tendrils of smoke rising from a smoldering stick. Candles adorned the table and provided a soft glow to the room and a subtle sparkle to the shimmering fabric that adorned the walls. Two carved wooden armchairs with plump cushions on the seats and backs sat facing each other.

"Please sit down," Cassandra waved her arm to indicate where she wanted Heather seated. Cassandra always sat in the East, her power center, and clients opposite her to the West. "What is your name?"

"Heather. I know that you're Cassandra, at least according to the sign. I've never done this before," said Heather. "I don't know what to expect."

"I will guide you through the process. Your role is to relax and focus on your questions. Take a deep breath and let it out slowly, then we may begin."

Heather did as she was told. The act of breathing let out the tension she felt as thoughts of Victoria swirled in her mind.

Cassandra pushed a deck of cards toward her. "Pick up the deck and shuffle the cards. Think of things you want to know about."

Heather shuffled. The cards were larger than a deck of playing cards, and she found them awkward to manipulate. She thought of Victoria and the invitation to dinner. Pictures of friends gathered around her and laughter and camaraderie came floating into her mind. She put the cards down on the table. Cassandra spread them in a wide arc and asked her to choose seven cards from anywhere in the deck. When finished, she handed them to Cassandra, who laid them out in several rows, the cards touching one another at the corners. The vibrant colors of the cards and the mysterious pictures captivated Heather and drew her in.

"Do you want to know my question?" asked Heather.

"We start by allowing the Universe to provide its message, and then we can ask specific questions."

Cassandra began to read the cards. "The five of wands comes up in the center, indicating that you will be getting involved with a group of people. The High Priestess is attached to this card. You have found someone who has great wisdom to share."

Heather was floored, wondering how she knew, but unable to say anything. Her eyes fell on a card that said, "Death." She gasped, worried at the implications. Cassandra continued.

"Death is a very misunderstood card. Have no fear of it. It indicates that a new cycle is upon you, an ending to a disagreeable situation. The Sun is attached to it, showing that the new circumstances will be better for you. You will have renewed energy and vitality."

Heather let out a relieved breath and smiled.

"The Fool is touching The Sun. It is time for you to take a leap of faith to begin your new life. By doing so, you will be on the path to positive change. You are at the beginning of a highly significant phase and great change is coming. The Knight of Wands appears with the High Priestess. He is a new man coming into your life that will help guide you on your journey."

"A boyfriend?" hoped Heather.

"Not initially at least. I'm not getting a sexual relationship with him, but he will play an important role in your transition. That doesn't mean it isn't possible; it just means that your relationship with him will be central to your transformation."

Heather remained hopeful that this new relationship would include love. She never had a boyfriend before.

"The last card is The Star. There is a draining of energy indicated here, either yours or someone else's. The pouring out of energy needs to be curtailed. When you feel weak, seek out ways to replenish your life force before it is completely drained. The new condition should do much to help with that. At the same time, it is important to be mindful of how you are feeling and to monitor your energy and that of others." Cassandra took a breath. "What questions do you have?"

"None. You've answered them all," Heather said in amazement. "Thank you so much."

"I hope it was helpful."

"More than you know." Heather paid for her session and left.

Cassandra sat at the table feeling quite tired. She had grounded herself that morning as she did before beginning readings for the day. She knew that the last client had pulled on her energy, taking more than Cassandra wanted to give. Heather's aura was riddled with holes and looked like a Dalmatian with spots of dark and light, reflecting her neediness and low energy. Heather's energy was leaking from her eroding aura, and she was trying to stop the seepage with Cassandra's energy. Cassandra did not get the sense that Heather was maliciously taking her energy; it seemed an unconscious act, unable to stop herself. Cassandra had to concentrate so as not to allow the vision of this odd aura to distract her. Healing energy could have been applied to Heather to close the holes, but Cassandra did not perform this type of service without permission. Given that this was Heather's first foray into the psychic realm, Cassandra felt it best to mention it if and when Heather returned. She did not want to tread in places the client was not yet ready to go.

She was compelled to smudge the reading room, as Heather had left a puddle of dark energy on the chair that she needed to clear before her next client arrived. As she maneuvered the smoke around the room with concentration on the chair, the smoke pooled over where Heather sat, necessitating a banishing prayer be said in addition to the smoke. Cassandra was finally able to dispel the negativity.

She had received more information than she imparted to Heather. There was a sense that she needed to be careful with this client. The people she had seen around her were powerful and potentially lethal to anyone other than Heather. For Heather, they would give her the guidance she longed for and needed, but they would benefit as well.

These players were not in it to develop Heather as an act of goodwill. When she had pulled information from The High Priestess card, she experienced the sensation of someone watching her. It felt different than the energy of a spirit entity and was difficult to identify. She had gotten a cold feeling, a warning of sorts, but was uncertain what to make of it. Cassandra's role as the reader was not to judge, but to objectively impart information. She had held back information that she was feeling within herself and not necessarily pertinent to Heather's inquiry. There was a fine line that was drawn when receiving and providing information. Still, Cassandra was unable to shake the sense of foreboding Heather's reading had left her with. She needed to cleanse herself of the session, and nothing did that better than a walk in the woods. With solid bookings for the rest of the afternoon, she promised herself to set off for the hiking trails first thing in the morning.

* * *

Victoria's trance was broken as Heather closed the door to Cassandra's psychic den. She had astrally followed Heather since she left the shop. The reading dispelled Heather's doubt, pushing Heather closer to her, and that pleased her. Heather's excursion into Cassandra's mystical world also gave Victoria a much-needed piece of information: She had found Iman.

Iman was born at dawn, the bringer of faith. Her allegiance was with the East, the element of Air, and the Wind of Renewal. Her parents were devout worshippers of Mithras, the strongest believers in the power of their god. They were honored to create a child for such a significant role in the service of the temple, and she glowed with a heavenly light. With blonde hair and blue eyes, she was an unusual treasure with her fair complexion. Her purpose was to bestow a belief in that which cannot be seen: the Source and its power.

In the present, Cassandra still embodied all that her ancient teacher had instilled. As Iman, the Elders selected Huda to be her teacher, a teacher possessing the ability to bestow the power of forgiveness and who was renowned for her energetic work with nature. They knew that she would provide the right guidance for Iman that would help her to reach her full, shining potential. She taught the child how to renew her own energy from things in nature, such as trees and bodies of water. Her lessons included energetic healing modalities and how to maintain the strength of the healer's body.

Iman became adept at diagnosing illness by seeing into the patient's auric field, then applying the correct energetic vibration to dissolve the anomaly. She also had the gift of divination, and could use both man-made and natural tools to gain profound insight into people and situations. Iman was never one to be ostentatious; Victoria was not surprised to find her in a small studio where she performed energetic healing and professional tarot readings. Victoria did not want to be recognized and would keep her distance from the studio for now. The spell of forgetting she had cast was still upon Iman and the others, but Victoria could feel its threads beginning to unravel. She turned her attention to Ethan.

* * *

The brief visit with Victoria gave Ethan something to focus on. She directed him toward a purpose, to find recruits for the coven, and gave him understanding about what he was seeing. It was a relief to know that there was nothing wrong with his eyes, so on the way to work, he practiced looking at people and objects. Plants had solid green auras, while people had all different colors and textures. It was hard to concentrate on one person at a time, especially when they walked close together. This would take practice. He took his time on the short walk to work from Victoria's shop.

The restaurant had an unusual look to it today. Ethan looked around. Nothing had changed. The décor was the same, the furniture, the Friday night shift workers, all the same. He realized the difference was in how the place *felt*. It was not only the building itself, but also the people. Cynthia, one of the waitresses, walked by him and gave him a wink. She had been after him for quite a while, hoping to be one of his many conquests, thinking she was woman enough to change him. He had been able to perceive her sexuality, her desire, and picture the games they could play together. Today he sensed her, but not in a sexual way. He picked up on her loneliness, her failed hopes of becoming a professional artist, and the low vibration of her energy field.

Ethan was out of his element and felt conflicted. He enjoyed the voyeuristic nature of his newly acquired ability, yet the unauthorized knowledge he was privileged to went against nature and, as such, should not be allowed to happen. To be exposed to others like that, to be read like an open book, would be devastating to Ethan. He felt a little guilty for peering into Cynthia's private thoughts, but only a little.

Never before had he known a low vibration from a high one. He and Cynthia had never discussed her aspirations or disappointments, yet he *knew*. There was no question in his mind that what he perceived was accurate. He turned his attention to Lynn, the owner of the restaurant. She was in her usual flurry of focused activity, readying the staff and herself for the Friday night dinner-and-drink crowd. The number of patrons sometimes as much as doubled on a weekend, and Lynn liked to be prepared. She was across the room from where he stood. He tried focusing on her as she flitted from one task to another. Nothing. Of all people, he wanted to know what his boss was thinking. Maybe there were too many people around. He tried to block them out. Still nothing. Frustration began to set in. Ethan determined that the distance from her prevented him from getting any information. He drew closer.

Lynn looked up from the register and waved in greeting. He waved back, training his eyes on her whole being. Ethan sensed her strength, resolve, and resistance to his invasion of her privacy. In the year he had been working for her, he had never seen her lose an argument or give in. Now he could *see* why. Her aura was solid, too solid for Ethan's fledgling skills to penetrate. His second effort to read her was unsuccessful, so he decided to move on to easier prey. It was valuable to explore his limitations. He promised himself he would work to overcome them and to hone his abilities.

He signed on to his shift, distracted by the energies he detected swirling around him. He had to get control over this. Odd that he did not feel this way when he was with Victoria earlier. He had not picked up anything from her. She was like a solid black wall to him, as the entire world had been only the night before.

As he went through the usual motions of his job that night, charming the ladies and catering to the gents, he observed his customers with new eyes. He was less distracted when he concentrated on one person or couple at a time; otherwise the barrage of information caused so much noise in his head, he could hear nothing else. The difference between weak and strong individuals was astounding. There were variations in texture and density. He sensed the underlying distress of a customer hidden by the smile she projected at her date. One diner beamed a strong field around himself, thoroughly enjoying the company of his wife and children. The boredom of a couple in the corner manifested as energy close to the surface of the skin.

Ethan was in a constant state of amazement at what he was experiencing. Part of him felt that he did feel this level of humanity in a more subtle way prior to his awakening. An instant aversion to certain people without apparent cause, fatigue around others, increased energy from some, was hinting at what waited to be discovered. Ethan's mind reeled at the possibilities. He was indebted to Victoria for choosing him for this honor.

His mind turned to the women he knew in the area who practiced Witchcraft. There were many, and he had met a couple of them one night drinking at the bar. If he could recruit them to join Victoria, he would elevate his status within the coven. This newfound perception was only the tip of the iceberg, and he wanted more.

* * *

Victoria laughed as she remotely listened to Ethan's plans of grandeur. It was simple to access his thoughts, so justified he felt in his ambitions. His progress would be limited, as superficiality does not lend itself well to the magical life. At least he was heading in the direction she wanted, with new recruits just days away. The goal was to acquire five total in the coven. Past experience showed that more than that created unwanted complications. Five was a good number to work with, as each could stand at a point of the pentagram, with Victoria at the head. Ethan would bring two to the fold, and Victoria would come across one. She felt her near—a desperate child, longing for companionship and guidance.

Victoria handled the vintage objects with great care and strategically placed them around the store. Some of the items were more valuable than others from a monetary perspective; others held mystical potency meant for specific individuals. Victoria had charged some of the pieces herself, anticipating the arrival of certain individuals. These objects would draw the appropriate person; someone who required its special brand of energy. One of the objects was from ancient times, meant to draw out the one she sought. Of the three she followed through time, Uzma had proven to be the most powerful.

Victoria dusted the treasures that served as bait to the unsuspecting.

* * *

Ethan kept checking the bar to see if his potential recruits had wandered in. They were bound to come back in at some point; he knew them to be regulars. A picture of Sandy came to mind, her shoulder-length blonde hair streaked with blue, purple, and black and wearing a pentagram necklace. Not at all like Victoria, whose power was present without the obvious markings of a Witch. His thoughts reverted to Helen, with her long, dark hair reaching the small of her back in one solid color. She generally wore black clothing. Paired with her aversion to the sun, the contrast of dark hair and clothing with her milky skin reminded him of Morticia Addams. The two were obviously pursuing the lifestyle of a witch. Would Victoria approve of so blatant a duo? Ethan would have to consider their energetic impressions before introducing them to his High Priestess. This was his opportunity to show Victoria that she could trust his judgment.

As Ethan had hoped, Sandy and Helen made an appearance around 10 pm, immersed in their usual Witchy image. They saw him look over, and they waved and smiled. Ethan was on the other side of the restaurant, too far to get a good read on the girls. His section was full, so had to wait another hour before the dinner crowd thinned out. He closed out his last customer and went to join them at the bar.

Sandy and Helen's blatant Witchy style made them novices in Ethan's mind. At the same time, their dark fashion sense was certainly appropriate for their jobs at Against the Grain, the best Medieval shop in the area, and Gypsy Heaven, a Witch supply shop. As he drew closer to the women, his new sight kicked in, and he saw he had been mistaken. Their auras were exceedingly strong and mingled together, yet touched no other in the room. The bond between them created a protective bubble. The shield was so solid; he was unable to read anything about them. It was apparent that he was the novice in this group.

"Did you change your hair or something?" Sandy asked Ethan and gave him a peck on the cheek. "You're handsome as ever, but something is different about you."

"I haven't changed a thing on the outside," Ethan stated the truth.

"All change comes from within," smiled Helen and kissed him on the other cheek.

"So what sparked your change, Ethan?" inquired Sandy.

Ethan smiled, "Victoria."

"Yeah, nothing like a new love interest to get the internal flame burning," said Helen.

"She's not a girlfriend," corrected Ethan. "She's my High Priestess."

"A convert!" exclaimed Sandy with delight. "You've come over to the world of witchery, have you?"

"It came as a surprise to me as well. It's not like I planned it. She was having dinner here last night and approached me about it. She owns Victoria's Antiques on Main Street. I'd love for you two to meet her. She's new to the area and starting a coven," Ethan explained. "Since I'm new to all of this, tell me a little about what you do as Witches."

"I'm a Green Witch," explained Helen. "My power and conjurations are attached to nature. I read signs from animals and plants and draw energy from them. I follow the currents of natural tides like lunar cycles and seasons and use them to do my Craft work."

"My specialty is protective magic," said Sandy. "I focus on psychic self-defense and dispelling negativity. Spells and rituals are formulated to go against the Dark Arts."

"Impressive. I didn't know you could specialize. Are you members of a coven?"

"We've always been primarily solitary practitioners. Group workings can get a little complicated," said Sandy.

"It would be great to start practicing The Craft with people I'm familiar with. Any chance you'd be open to joining Victoria's coven?"

"As Sandy said, we don't do group work. I'm not sure we're into joining a coven," agreed Helen.

"You can always meet Victoria and decide if she's someone you'd like to get involved with," Ethan coaxed. "Besides, you could always do it as a favor to me."

"Lesson one to the newly initiated: Magical workings are not done as a favor or taken lightly. Every action taken has consequences. Consider what you are asking for with every thought and conjuration and the potential ramifications. It's called the Law of Attraction. You attract what you think about; your thoughts impact your destiny. Say you saw a woman you wanted, but she wasn't interested in you..." Sandy instructed.

"Not likely," said Ethan with a smile, "I haven't struck out yet."

"Humor me for a moment," said Sandy, shaking her head at his conceit. "You cast a love spell to make her want to be with you. The spell works, and she wants to be with you all the time. You need space and don't want her there every minute. She begins to stalk you, her desire to be with you overwhelming your request for some privacy."

"That would be a nightmare," Ethan shivered at the thought of a woman constantly with him, watching his every move. "I get your meaning, but what harm would it do to have dinner with a friend and maybe even make a new one?"

"I guess it couldn't hurt to meet her. The spirits will guide us toward her or away." Helen gave in.

"Okay, just let us know when," Sandy said with a sigh and a shrug. She gave Ethan their business cards: Sandy's for *Gypsy Heaven* and Helen's for *Against the Grain*.

"I'll check with Victoria to confirm a date and time. We can just have dinner to start with," Ethan promised. He pictured Victoria rewarding his recruiting efforts. These two would be potent additions to the group.

Hiding their trepidation about the upcoming gathering, the three sat at the bar laughing and talking until last call at 2 am.

⇍ **3** ⇍

Cassandra got an early start on her walk in the woods. Early morning was a glorious time to be in the awesome presence of grand old trees, sunlight filtered by the massive leaf canopies of late summer foliage. The quiet was church-like at that hour, the foot traffic was sparse, and the birds and animals provided their sacred stirrings in the forest. Victoria watched with closed eyes as Cassandra left her bungalow and headed for the hiking trails nearby.

The entrance to the woods welcomed her. Cassandra opened herself to the energy around her to gather information on which to base her prophesies. Beginning with a visual scan of the surroundings, Cassandra opened her third eye to glimpse the forest before her. She loved to walk through the woods and look at the deep green auric field that emanated from every leaf and branch. Cassandra used the solid energy of the trees to replenish her own diminished resources. Heather had taken too much strength from her, leaving her uncharacteristically tired.

She extended her arms to touch the auric field of the ancient oak and maple trees that lined the asphalt path through the park. A slight breeze brushed her long blonde hair back from her face and shoulders, and she reveled in its touch. Cassandra drew the abundant vitality from these stationary beings into the palms of her hands and let it wash over her entire body. She allowed the life force to flow into her, feeling it swirl around her solar plexus. The sensation reminded her of being on a roller coaster on the descending portion of its journey. Focused in her mid-torso, the spirits of the trees manifested as butterflies in her stomach. Cassandra had achieved total connection to the benevolent energy source.

Her bright blue eyes fell upon the lacy fern, dirt mounds with moss and old tree branches. She allowed her feet to follow a winding forest path she had never noticed before, watching squirrels running around trees and seeing the tips of their tails around the bend. She liked how life sprung forth from the dead, decaying tree trunks. Sunlight spotted the trail through the dense canopy of trees. Two deer munched on tender leaves a few yards away from the trail, blending into the forest background and looking at her to determine if she was a threat. Bowing their heads to get another mouthful of green leaves signaled their decision.

Cassandra never feared getting lost for she could hear the rushing of the creek over the stones from most paths in the forest even when she could not see it. The path was carved into steep hills covered in crushed stone. Crows flew overhead bringing a message. Magic was afoot – what type was to be determined. Grape vines twisted down from the treetops. A lone wild turkey poked his way through the deep grasses. She wondered why it was alone; that was unusual. Coming around the bend, she saw its companion.

A smaller trail went into the woods from the main trail. Branches had fallen from a large tree, making a welcoming gateway into a private grove. Surrounded by fallen trees covered in thick vines, she entered the natural nook, loving the seclusion, protection, and privacy it offered. A large tree was in the middle of it, its roots reaching around the grove twisting and digging into the rich soil. A small white-bellied bird with a sharp, pointy beak hopped from one branch to another.

She paused to feel the magic in the copse, testing it with the amethyst pendulum she always brought with her on these journeys through the forest. The bullet-shaped stone was suspended from a thin chain. It picked up the flow of energy in the copse and responded in a clockwise arc, indicating positive vibrations, tracing a perfect circle in the air without prompting from Cassandra's hand. This spot had powerful energy as she suspected. She returned the pendulum to its small velvet pouch and shoved it back into the front pocket of her jeans.

She spotted a spirit opening between two thin young maples draped heavily with leaved vines in the shape of a smile. Only nature spirits could enter here. The doorway was too high at the bottom for humans to walk over; hence only woodland spirits could go through. Wild roses, scattered here and there, demonstrated their thorny beauty. Chipmunks scampered across the path and behind a log. They moved so fast. There was enchantment at every turn. Cassandra took it in all at once and entered a state of intense awareness and an overall sensation of calm. The joy flooded her heart, opening her chakras to a deep sense of peace and contentment.

At home in the woods, her psychic cells were supercharged and tingling. Her aura touched everything around her, comprehending the total beauty of the forest in every fiber of her being. The fallen, decaying trunks of the Old Ones, pouring their energy back into the surroundings for the benefit of the survivors. The soft, green moss, the towering maple trees, and the delicate fern were decorating the landscape and providing a cohesive symmetry to the scene. In adulthood, as in childhood, her protection came from the Universal Energy, the sacred force that sent its beacon across the planet, fortifying and connecting all living things. She felt this unifying vitality the strongest in the presence of trees.

As early as two years old, Cassandra could remember feeling a connection to trees. She would play contentedly next to the largest tree in her yard, until her mother would come and get her. She made sure that her sandbox was located under that tree. Cassandra preferred shade to sunlight and, as she grew older, spent much time walking in the woods alone. Sometimes she would ride her bike. There were times when she would invite a friend or two to join her, but these excursions did not hold the same enjoyment. The chatter and activity of others diminished the experience. Unable to feel the energy of the trees as intensely when others were present, Cassandra no longer allowed friends to tag along.

On the playground at recess, Cassandra could be found sitting next to a large oak tree with a skull and cross-bones carved into its bark. She could not understand who would want to hurt her beloved tree in that way. By staying nearby the injured being, she hoped to give some healing back to it. The children in her class thought she was strange, commenting to each other on how Cassandra preferred to be alone. Books and trees became her favorite companions, occasionally tolerating one or two of her schoolmates for a limited time. Not only did she find that children were cruel to each other, and sometimes to her, but their energy served to agitate her. Being close to the auric fields of these children opened her to a considerable amount of static energy that became unbearable at times. Her only escape was to separate herself from them. Adults had a lesser effect, as their electromagnetic fields and psychic abilities had dissipated over time.

It wasn't until Cassandra began her formal energy work that she learned to properly ground. This technique enabled her to be around people for extended periods of time. Crowds, however, were still undesirable. It was more difficult to maintain a shield against the negative energies when they were coming at her in a great mass. Over time, she discovered that most adults were unaware of their own energy field, not to mention the auric fields of others. Children were much more in tune with themselves and the Universal energy that flowed freely around them. They even experimented with throwing that energy in focused bursts to see what would happen.

Until this realization and ability to control the absorption of the negative life force of others, Cassandra was labeled as "unusual" and "unsociable." Her parents had never taken the time to intervene, since she was a quiet child who was adept at occupying herself. This freed her parents to go on through their daily routine with no fear of disruption from her. Alone, she was unrestricted in her study and practice of white magic. Some of her research paper topics were somewhat disturbing to her teachers, such as her treatise about the Salem witch trials. She defended it by saying that it was a legitimate, historical event. The teacher could not argue the point, but commented that the subject was quite morbid and offered that she may wish to choose a more cheerful theme for her next paper. This comment did not dissuade her from doing a paper on the practice of Voodoo when the class did a unit on Haiti, much to her teacher's dismay.

Cassandra's fascination with the supernatural was steadfast, and she read all the books she could find on the subject. Ghosts, levitation, spirituality, metaphysics, extrasensory perception, and religion began to cluster in her mind to develop into her notion of how she fit into the Universe. The nature of her powers revealed itself to her gradually, showing up at unsolicited times. She was never sure when her psychic ability would come forth. It became her goal to observe and record the times that it surfaced. Cassandra realized that her psychic peaks occurred in autumn, with October being her strongest month.

With autumn around the cosmic corner of the wheel of the year, the cooler weather was only weeks away. It would prompt her to venture outdoors more often after hiding from the heat and the sun of summer, to revel in the beauty of the magnificent colors of fall. The sight of the leaves dripping from the trees in shades of red, orange, and yellow filled her with awe. Cassandra anticipated the sound of the crunching leaves as she glided down the wooded path, mingling with the chirping of the last birds; these sounds played music to her finely tuned ears. The earthy fragrance of the autumn woods made her lightheaded, and she looked forward to the coming change of season. A tingle suddenly passed through her, sending waves of cold to her hands and feet. She looked around to see where the sudden stab of energy had come from, but saw nothing. Shaking it off, she returned to thoughts of autumn.

New Hope, Pennsylvania, was famous for its fall foliage, and her small abode took advantage of the views that the town offered. It was fitting for Cassandra's three-bedroom bungalow to be nestled in a grove of hundred-year-old maples with a brook flowing at the rear of her property. Quaint shops were abundant, including those selling metaphysical paraphernalia and supplies to accommodate the town's

Witchcraft practitioners. There was no shortage of folks in the vicinity who were involved in the pursuit of psychic awareness and strength. Readers of palms, Tarot cards, tealeaves, and energy left on objects, known as psychometrists, had shops on every other block. Her own practice was blessedly successful, as word of her talent passed from customers to their friends. Several private bookstores were located in the town. Restaurants offered casual and formal atmospheres and served a wide variety of food and drink.

Originally from the New York City area with its heavy traffic and high noise level, Cassandra felt much more at home in this bustling, historic little town. Her sacred trees were plentiful, and the local residents had accepted her. She had made a couple of very good friends who shared her interests and who understood her power and their own. Free to practice her craft and to roam the woods, Cassandra felt as though she had found a sanctuary. To say it was heavenly would also be accurate, although her belief system did not incorporate the mythical places of Heaven and Hell. Tied to the Universe as she was, Cassandra understood that those places were symbolic, existing primarily as dichotomous aspects of the self.

Walking, peacefully connected to her surroundings, Cassandra caught a glimpse of someone wearing white standing in a grove of trees about fifty feet from her. She turned to give a smile, for she always acknowledged fellow woods walkers. The trees stood alone to accept her greeting. Scanning the area, she realized that a spirit of some type had joined her on her walk. The same sensation she felt when reading Heather returned, a foreboding sensation that made her body tingle with cold. She continued on, now aware of her ethereal companion, yet unaware that it was Victoria Perry, who watched with an astral eye.

Fully charged, Cassandra exited the woods, off to join her friends. She looked forward to Sunday brunch with Macy and Alexis. They had met about five years ago in a local New Age shop called *Mystickal Tymes*. They thought it was their common interest in divination, spirituality, and energy work that bonded them to a life-long friendship, still unaware of their history together. Their connection allowed them to communicate with each other without speaking. Whenever something was wrong with one of them, the other two would know. If they were engaged in a casual conversation, they were able to complete each other's sentences.

Today they were meeting at the Logan Inn, where they could eat outside under the protection of a striped awning. Cassandra was first to arrive and stood outside at the old cannon in front of the Inn, waiting for the others. Main Street was busy today, filled with cars and motorcycles attempting to secure a parking space. Pedestrians swarmed on the sidewalks, leisurely walking from shop to shop and trying to decide the type of cuisine to enjoy. Twinkle lights glistened in the trees and decorated the storefronts that were lit despite the full daylight, waiting for the sun's demise. Twilight in New Hope always had a magical feeling to it. There was an air of expectation that something miraculous was about to occur.

Cassandra stood patiently waiting, watching the activity around her, and saw Alexis hurry down the path toward the cannon, hating to be late, disliking making others wait. Her chestnut hair flew behind her. Cassandra focused her attention on Alexis, her casual outlook reflected in her attire of jeans and a simple black top, rather than the hoards of people around her. When she got together with Macy and Alexis, her auric field opened only to them. Their energies were linked. She knew it from the first time they met that they were destined to be together. Basking in the light of that friendship was a welcome feeling, giving her a break from opening to people with personal issues and serious problems. She enjoyed her work as a professional Tarot reader and Reiki practitioner. It allowed her to help people and provide spiritual support and enlightenment to those who needed it most. At the same time, Cassandra had to give herself what she needed, and that was a break from the drama and negativity that was inherent in her work.

Macy took quick, deliberate steps as she pranced down the sidewalk and past the many enticing shops that lined Main Street. She couldn't resist window shopping and made a mental note to see if the ladies would like to circle back and check out the new antique shop. She spotted Cassandra and Alexis embracing next to the historic cannon at the intersection of Main and Ferry Streets, a block away from where she was. It could have been a mile away and she still would have recognized those two. The energy that flowed between them was unmistakable, smooth and joined; it exemplified a genuine unity of two spirits. Macy's spirit lifted, knowing that her own aura would be mingled with theirs momentarily. Few people were pleasant to be with. Alexis and Cassandra were always comfortable to be around. There was no posturing necessary, no defensiveness, just straight up friendship. There was nothing that Macy hesitated to share with them.

With her friends in view, Macy was suddenly hit with an unexplained compulsion to surround them in a protective shell of white light, spurred on by a distant presence. She had a chill and looked around to see if she was being watched. Expanding her gaze to the area on either side of Cassandra and Alexis, Macy saw nothing that would have indicated that they were threatened in any way. Her experience taught her long ago not to question psychic impulses, so she beamed out a thick, bright shield that encapsulated her beloved friends.

Two sets of open arms welcomed her, and with perfect love and perfect trust, she entered the circle of friendship.

* * *

Victoria's view of the women was suddenly and completely cut off, but not before she recognized Uzma and Mina. The power of the protective shield that had severed her vision could only come from Uzma.

Uzma was the most potent of all; her power felt as she emerged from her mother's womb. The flame of her red hair and bewitching green eyes punctuated the fire of her spirit. Uzma, emerged at noon, and her name reflected her nature as supreme or greatest among them. Uzma was aligned with the energies of the South; the element of Fire and the Winds of Change and Energy were her allies. Uzma's mother and father held high-ranking positions in the temple and were trusted members of the community. Their contributions to the laws governing their city and the temple were developed with a sense of fairness and concern for all citizens. They intended for Uzma to become an ethical and righteous leader, her reign an outgrowth of the desires of her fellow temple dwellers.

Victoria remembered Uzma' teacher, Akilah. She was the perfect choice to instruct Uzma about The Seven Fires, the charm against the Seven Evil Spirits. Akilah had exceptional talent in using the rituals in the Maqlu text to counter negative spells. The Maqlu's purpose was to protect against—or, if necessary, destroy—evil sorcerers. Uzma was extraordinarily receptive and developed the ability to read information contained in any object. She could also sense the thoughts of others.

Akilah knew that Uzma was destined to be the leader of the group and that her power would not be abused. Victoria had pangs of jealousy haunt her friendship with Uzma, knowing she would not be the one to take the leadership role. It was disappointing to Qadir as well. The force that emanated from Uzma was pure and strong, and Akilah armed her with all the tools she needed to defend the scrolls and herself against negative attacks; so there was little Victoria or Qadir could do to change the course of fate. Victoria had the greatest respect for Uzma and at the same time held the most contempt for her. She posed the greatest threat to Victoria.

Mina had always amused Victoria. She was the most innocent of the four. Through Iman, Victoria derived her name in this life to be Alexis.

Born along with the others in 371 A.D, the name Mina represented the gemstone lapis lazuli, which was imbedded on the image of the Moon God Sin. The name also denoted the role of protector. Aligned with the West, the element of Water, and the Wind of Love and Fertility, she had been given the gifts of spirit contact and seeing into the future. Her time of power was Twilight. Her parents were the most nurturing of the priests and priestesses and doted on her. Mina was aligned with the full moon, and learned to use its power to conjure her desires and the desires of others. Victoria remembered how her chestnut hair and large brown eyes glowed in moonlight, effortlessly absorbing its energy.

The Elders selected Hala to teach her about moon phases and other spellcraft correspondences, especially herbs and gemstones. Hala was well known for her affinity for the moon and was thought to have a seat beside Sin, the moon god, when it was her time to cross over. Mina acclimated to her lessons immediately, reveling in the moonlight and the powerful feeling it provided. Her knowledge of appropriate correspondences to enhance the power of her spells was unparalleled, exceeding even that of her teacher. Mina's ability to foresee future events and to pick up subtle vibrations assisted her in acquiring valuable information. Hala and Mina became very attached and spent countless hours together.

Victoria knew that she missed having a teacher and would be searching for one in this lifetime. She planned to fill that void for her.

* * *

Despite the crowd, which was to be expected on any weekend day, the hostess was able to seat them quickly. After ordering the buffet and drinks, they settled in to plan the remainder of their day together. Activities were always flexible, each throwing out their preference.

"It looks like *Mystickal Tymes* has some new items in the window. I passed it on the way over," Alexis said.

"I saw that, too. I'd also like to stop in that new antique store that just opened up down the street," Macy offered.

"I'm not in the mood for antiques today," said Alexis, with Cassandra nodding her head in agreement.

"How about I go and check it out, then I'll meet you two at *Mystickal Tymes?*"

"Sounds good to me!" Alexis said with relief.

They got up to load their plates at the extensive buffet. An hour later, full, and ready to shop, the women separated to check out various stores. Macy headed to the antique store that was calling to her.

Victoria watched from the shadows of the back room as Macy entered, allowing her the space to explore on her own, confident she would find the piece Victoria displayed for her alone. Macy could feel her dark gaze. The discomfort Macy felt did not deter her from the exquisite items she saw. Macy stopped to consider a shiny bronze urn that rested on three gently curved legs. Handles of intricately molded snakes caressed either side of the urn's body. The vented brass lid was topped with a miniature lion. It was difficult to determine the age of the piece.

The piece had a strong presence. Macy thought it perfect to burn copal resin on charcoal disks. She pictured thick curls of fragrant smoke wafting through the lid. She continued to feel eyes on her. Macy reached out to check the hand-written price tag hanging from a string taped to the underbelly of the censer. It was reasonable at thirty dollars. She closed her fingers around each well-formed handle. Victoria watched Macy's reaction as she touched the incense burner. Macy's expression tightened and brow furrowed as she gripped the snake handles of the ceremonial urn; she was in the throes of a vision. Uzma had always been a powerful psychometrist, and Victoria was able to share her experience as she picked up the vibrations that revealed the urn's history.

Sparks burned through Macy's skin and up her arms. An altar filled with dozens of flickering candles and several ornamental brass incense urns flashed in Macy's mind. She could see the soft glow of the tiny flames waving across the ancient stone backdrop that lined the chamber. A blue Spirit Flame burned as the altar's centerpiece. Her senses alerted her to the presence of three others sitting in a half moon in front of the altar. They were silent in their focused contemplation. Their energy in unison created a thickness in the air. *We've prayed together often*, Macy thought. It was obvious that Macy was having a powerful vision and Victoria instantly regretted putting the urn on display. Did Macy realize that it was a memory? Would she recall the scrolls?

Still holding the brass snakes, Macy felt herself step toward the altar. Looking down, she saw a black flowing skirt fluttering with each barefoot step closer to the altar. Her arms up, her thumbs resting on top of her head, her fingers forming a triangle. It was a necessary gesture to summon the power of The Great One. Macy kneeled on one of the raw silk pillows scattered like autumn leaves in front of the altar. She felt reverence for what was about to happen. She was the conduit for their focused attention. Through her, *it* would manifest. Her inner strength would withstand the energy that was about to pass through her.

Victoria decided that it was time to step in.

"Can I help you?" Victoria said in a low, authoritative voice that disrupted Macy's vision. Macy was yanked into the present, once again aware of the cool metal on her skin. She felt as though emerging from a dream, groggy with memories from another time. Her eyes beheld the source of the revelation. The urn had to be hers. She would take it home and complete the ceremony she saw in the vision. Macy was now unsure of her true identity. Her sense of self was altered by the clear memory of a former incarnation.

"I'll take this," she said, handing the urn to Victoria.

"Will that be all?" she pressed, knowing that Macy had made her only selection of the evening.

Victoria allowed Macy the privacy of her thoughts as the credit card transaction was processed.

"How long has this store been open?" asked Macy.

"I opened a few days ago," answered Victoria.

"I'm glad I found you before the urn was sold to someone else," Macy said.

"It was meant to be," said Victoria, as she wrapped the purchase in tissue and placed it in a brown paper bag hand-stamped with a coiling snake design. "I hope to see you again," she said with a sly smile and unwavering gaze.

I'm sure you will, thought Macy. With the otherworldly episode clinging to her mind's eye, Macy took her prize with a polite *thank you* and walked quickly out of the store.

Victoria did not worry about the deeper revelations to come. The stress of deception and betrayal had started to wear on her, and she wondered if subconsciously she wanted the final confrontation to occur. Seeking power over others was quite exhausting.

Macy hurried to join her friends at *Mystickal Tymes*. They were in the divination section, laughing and showing each other various volumes.

Cassandra noticed the bag. "What did you find?" she inquired.

"A bronze incense holder," Macy minimized the importance of the piece.

"You're sweating. Are you feeling all right?" asked Alexis.

"Yes, I'm okay. Did you two find anything interesting?" Macy was eager to get off the subject. She did not want to share such an important experience until they were able to have privacy.

Cassandra and Alexis played along and showed Macy items throughout the store. They knew that something was wrong and allowed Macy to skirt the issue. Macy asked them to join her for breakfast at her home the next morning. They readily agreed, anxious to know what was going on.

≈ 4 ≈

The Labor Day holiday weekend afforded Monday off from work, allowing Macy to have her friends over for breakfast. The unconventional energy brought by the moon sitting in Aquarius was a perfect backdrop for the adventure on which they were about to embark.

The smell of fresh-brewed French vanilla coffee permeated the air and the sound of rain played its gentle music on the green leaves and slate rooftop of the massive English Tudor. Macy cherished this type of day off. Damp and dreary to many, this weather conjured happy memories of childhood, safe and warm in the reading nook Macy's parents had designed especially for her. Bookshelves were constructed on either side of the window seat to hold all of Macy's treasured volumes, both fiction and non-fiction. A comfy cushion covered in iridescent burgundy silk was nestled against a divided-light bay window. She pretended she was reading from an elegant tree house, and the second floor location fed the fantasy.

In the octagonal glass breakfast nook, Macy sat at a round white marble table atop a thick cushion cradled by a white wrought iron chair. The glass enclosure brought about a sense of being both protected and exposed. Sipping coffee and reading the latest Anne Rice novel, she was surrounded by the natural art created by the dense forest of her backyard. The deep green leaves would soon be interspersed with red, gold, and orange, perched for one last ostentatious display before diving from their branches and floating down to the pool of moss below. The gray sky at midday promised that the rain would continue for several more hours. The warm, damp air outside amplified her sense of comfort inside the luxurious home.

The rain glistened and popped on the flagstone patio. Macy's peace was disrupted by the image of Victoria, watching her as she fondled the bronze urn in the antique store. The rain-soaked leaves became a backdrop as Macy remembered reaching out to touch the censer. Until now, the urn had stayed wrapped in paper. Macy wanted to be in a safe place for her journey. She was now prepared for her next encounter with the ceremonial incense pot. She reached out toward the ominous paper bag and gently opened its mouth. The rustle of paper announced the urn's emergence. A sense of excitement overtook her as she quickly removed the tissue from the base and lid. With the lid placed on its base, the incense pot stood proudly on its curved legs, taunting her. Macy repositioned herself in her chair, felt her feet on the floor, and took a deep breath.

Grasping the handles as though driving an out-of-control vehicle, Macy felt the world fall away. Once again she was in the land of warm shadows. She liked the silky feeling of the ceremonial robe against her skin. Surrounded by friends, she was content and comfortable. She was carrying the urn toward the altar. The long marble slab rested on two ornamental pillars. Its whiteness provided a canvas for the flickering candles and the gleam of the ritual tools. The silk drapes that softened the walls of stone rippled in the wake of her movement.

Macy placed the incense pot in its rightful place on the altar, and the ritual was ready to begin. The others stood simultaneously, rising slowly from their seated positions. They raised their arms toward the sky and opened their hands to pull in the Universal Energy. Eyes closed in reverent concentration, the energy poured through them, saturating their essence with protection and light. Macy lit the charcoal disk and placed copal resin in the urn, as her sisters took on an eerie glow. She replaced the lid and watched the thick, fragrant smoke drift through the grates. Macy turned to face the others. With head bowed and palms raised to the sky, she gathered her share of the powerful energy that beamed into the temple.

Amidst the fluttering silk and soaring pillars, the coven stood in silent worship, each member a glowing silo. Connected by an unseen thread, the women reached toward each other until their middle fingertips lightly touched. The completed circuit pushed the energy around the circle, charging each member one at a time, until all four were equally filled. Their heads fell back, closed eyes gazed at the ceiling. Together they pushed the energy up and out, beaming with a force that obliterated the shadows. They filled the sacred room with ethereal light, casting out negativity and creating a protective field.

As the women swirled energy through the chamber, Macy focused on the objects of their purpose—The Scrolls of the Four Winds. "Protect the scrolls and the wisdom that is held within. Protect the secret room where they rest. Guard the poison scroll that holds *The Seven Evil Spirits* and defend with its sacred antidote *The Seven Fires* when the time is right. Ensure they remain in close proximity. Surround the deadly text with white light to contain its destructive force. Allow us to always be together and continue as Watchers, providing protection for all four directions, to ensure the scrolls are secured, "Macy chanted. "Give us the Power of the Seven Fires to use in battle if it becomes necessary. This energy goes out with unlimited blessings."

The group launched the protective shield and directed it to surround the scrolls in a cocoon of energy. With the release of energy, the women sighed and lowered their arms to their sides. They tingled from the rush of energy they had channeled. Macy turned back to the altar and picked up a silver chalice filled with red wine. She took a sip and passed it to her chestnut-haired sister, Mina. *Alexis. How could it be?* Continuing the ceremony, she passed a plate of bread. It was necessary to eat after a ritual to reestablish a grounded connection to the earthly plane. The fair-haired sister, Iman, received the platter. *Cassandra. But who is the third? And what is that banging sound...?*

In reliving the primeval memory, Macy felt a longing for the group to reunite. She recognized Cassandra and Alexis, but could not focus in on the third group member. Macy decided that the three of them would combine their energies and put the puzzle pieces together. For the time being, the mystery member of the group remained shielded. What extraordinary power they wielded together!

The knock on the door came harder and pulled Macy from the ancient scene. The tingling sensation lingered. She pushed herself away from the table and fixed herself as she walked toward the front door. Macy saw Alexis and Cassandra through the peephole. "Good timing," said Macy and opened the door with a smile.

After pouring them some coffee and getting settled in the conservatory, Macy showed them the urn and told them about the visions. She described the scenario as a mysterious echo from the past. Alexis and Cassandra were interested in the role that they played in a time long ago that now whispered its secrets to Macy. They decided to focus together to tap into this ancient energy.

Cassandra pulled a dark purple velvet bag from her purse. She slid open the top, releasing the draw string, and pulled out a set of Tarot cards. Cassandra always carried a deck with her. Today she had chosen the Ancestral Path Tarot. Cassandra shuffled the cards, and then spread them across the table.

"Let's see what information we can pick up with the cards." She asked Alexis and Macy to pull five cards each. Cassandra pulled five for herself. "Turn them over in front of you. Put two at the top, one in the middle, and two at the bottom, with the corners touching." The cards depicted scenes from various civilizations throughout history: ancient Egypt, Native American, Medieval Europe, and Asia. "Don't concern yourself with the meanings of the cards. Relax and focus on them. Let them help to prompt a mental picture of the past."

Alexis was the first to get an image. She spoke in a slow, dreamy voice. "The soldiers admired our beauty as we boarded the ship. Each of us had a unique shade of long flowing hair in blonde, chestnut, black, and red. Around our heads we wore silver bands with the symbol of the crescent moon adorning our foreheads. We all wore the same form-fitting white gown of pure silk with long, pointed sleeves. The soft fabric outlining our gentle curves enticed the men even more. We did not make eye contact as we boarded, nor did they engage in conversation. No word was spoken out of apprehension of the consequences. Only the murmur of water against the vessel was heard. Our focus was dedicated to the scrolls. We were educated in the history and contents of the sacred scrolls and understood the grave importance of our mission.

"Spears and arrows ready, the army remained vigilant to attack. We were sacred human cargo that was to be guarded at all cost, no single life too precious to be sacrificed for the cause. We had traveled far across land along the trade route from Mesopotamia and now made our way across the Mediterranean Sea, destined for the Great Library of Alexandria in Egypt. The daylight would soon be gone, and our journey would continue through the moonlit night. The soldiers stood silent in their purpose and fearful of the power they protected. They had heard many stories of the Triad Witches and of their potent gifts."

Alexis remembered the desire in the soldiers' eyes, coupled with the fear of repercussion should the women decide to retaliate. The unsolicited adoration made her angry, but the others ignored them and remained focused. Alexis looked up at one of the soldiers, gazing at him through the chestnut-colored hair blowing across her face. He straightened and looked away, understanding the danger of persisting in his eternally unfulfilled fantasy.

The rain made soft rhythms as Cassandra continued the vision… "Seated below deck in a circle, we conjured an intense white light that was projected toward the ancient manuscripts housed miles away in the Great Library. The gentle rocking of the ship did not disturb our concentration as we beamed a circle of energy from one to the other, creating a solid barrier impenetrable by outside forces. The soldiers could see the glow that emanated from our sacred circle through the floorboards of the deck. The eerie light gave off a heat unlike any the men had ever felt: its intensity penetrating through the wood floor and pulsing into the bottoms of their feet."

Cassandra recalled the intensity of that night. Maintaining concentration, she, as Iman, looked at the other three witches. She respected their power and appreciated their beauty. They had been taught about the balance between light and darkness and had learned their lessons well. The light within her was glad to be associated with such a talented group. From out of the light, she saw a darkness emanating from one she did not recognize. Her name came through as Amira. She possessed an air of superiority and held bitterness and jealousy toward the other Witches. Cassandra could sense the resentment and sought to project kindness toward her sister to calm the anger.

Macy picked up on Cassandra's impressions. She, as Uzma, felt the intensity of their beam suddenly grow. "I see Amira sitting across from me with an eerie smile on her face, the sudden wave of light emanating from her. My name is Uzma, and my childhood friend Amira has been growing more and more distant from the group, frequently going off on her own rather than spending time with us. I had seen Amira walking in the garden with the evil priest, Qadir. For his crimes against the God of Light, Mithra, those against the Moon God, Nanna Sin, and his attack against a temple priest, he should have been banished from the order and from the community. Instead, the Council had forever denied him any elevation in rank. We were present when the High Priest issued his decree against Qadir. I watched as the darkness of his auric field clouded over and took on an added murkiness, as though his entire form was encrusted in mud. How he was able to move energy through the thick shadow of his aura was a mystery. I sensed that any light he was using to manifest his will was stained as it passed through the conduit of his tainted spirit. Now Amira's aura had begun to take on the same darkness Qadir possessed."

"We were witches! The Triad Witches! We were a coven!" exclaimed Alexis. "But if there were four of us, why were we called 'Triad?' Doesn't that mean three?"

"The number three is the number of manifestation and order, embodying the mind, body, and spirit. It is the mystic number of unity. Together, we were able to bring forth anything we desired. It has alchemical ties to the four elements of Earth, Air, Fire, and Water," said Macy, the knowledge coming through as second nature.

"We were friends and very powerful, trained to guard the sacred scrolls. I'd like to know more about those. My name was Iman. Macy was Uzma. But who is Amira? She is the only one in the vision that I do not recognize," pondered Cassandra.

"I recognize her," said Macy. "I believe she is the woman from the antique shop who sold me the incense burner." They sat in silence for a minute.

"My name didn't come through, and I couldn't see the fourth witch, but I knew she was there," said Alexis.

"You were Mina," said Macy. "It came through in the vision I had using the censer."

Ever the seeker of knowledge, Alexis's mind reeled with possibilities. "It would be great to pinpoint the time period when this took place. When did the Great Library exist? I know it was destroyed, but when and how, I'm not sure. We should try to look for clues in the visions. Let's try scrying for information. I have the mirror with me." Alexis had been practicing scrying techniques, attempting to see visions using a blackened mirror or dark bowl filled with water. By focusing on the reflective surface, it allows the mind to find the information sought after by the inquirer.

"What better place to find out about the Great Library than at a library? I'm sure the librarian there can point us to the texts that will help us to fill in the gaps. Try to get some information about the sacred scrolls as well," offered Cassandra.

"I'll go tomorrow," said Alexis.

That's enough remembering for one day. Let's eat. We can get together tomorrow to see if we can pick up anything else. How about dinner here?" They agreed.

The women were deep in thought as they departed into the rainy afternoon.

* * *

The rhythm of the rain on the store windows inspired Victoria as she set up her showroom by the light of small lamps she had lit around the store, their low wattage casting shadows on the floor and into the corners. The rain held mystical significance for her, cleansing and purifying on the one hand and a source of fertilization to promote growth on the other. The transforming power of the rain cooled the heat of the day and cast a shadow over the village. Her familiars liked the shadows, and came willingly. The sun dispelled their power, so they tended to appear reluctantly when she called under luminous conditions.

Macy and the others were tapping into information about the ancient past and soon the secret would once again be known. A figure moved in her peripheral vision waiting for her to glance over. She knew it was Qadir standing in the gloom of the corner before she moved her gaze toward him. Centuries of interaction made his energetic imprint familiar.

"The web is unraveling," he said in a low tone.

"Yes, they are starting to remember," Victoria quietly confirmed.

"We need their cooperation or the Scrolls of the Four Winds will remain inaccessible to us."

"Put your trust in me," she said without challenge.

"If you are not successful, trust that the punishment will last beyond any I have exacted in the past," Qadir promised.

"I understand," Victoria said as she hung her head.

≈ 5 ≈

The phone rang at 9 am, way before Ethan was scheduled to wake for the day. His restaurant job had put his body on a late day to late evening schedule. He tried to sound awake as he answered the phone.

"Ethan Talbot, please," the unfamiliar, somewhat sterile female voice said.

"This is Ethan," he replied.

"My name is Sonya Haverly. I am a recruiter for the Sandlock Corporation. We are in receipt of your resume and would like you to come in for an interview today at 1 pm. Are you available?"

"I'll be there," he tried to contain his excitement.

"Great. Please come to the main entrance and let the receptionist know when you arrive. She will direct you to my office."

"Thank you very much. I look forward to meeting you, Ms. Haverly," Ethan said in his best professional voice.

"See you at 1 pm, Mr. Talbot," she hung up.

Ethan was pleased, and only partially surprised. Victoria had cast the spell that got him the interview, but would it do the whole job and land him the position? He knew he would have to put effort into it as well and not simply rely on magic. Showered and looking dapper in his best gray suit, Ethan wished it were not raining. The weather did not slow him down, and he showed up 15 minutes early for his appointment. The receptionist welcomed him as he shook off his umbrella and put it in the stand next to the door. With a comment on the foul weather, she offered him a seat to wait.

Sonya Haverly came down at 1:10 pm, apologizing for her lateness. Ethan followed her to her office on the second floor.

"You submitted your resume a while back, and I'm not sure how it was overlooked. Your qualifications are exactly what we've been looking for. I'd like you to meet the vice president who is hiring for this position," she said while peering at him over her reading glasses. She called Bill Jenkins to make sure he was in his office to receive Ethan. Sonya stood and asked Ethan to follow her down the hallway. So far, he did not need to use his charm on Sonya.

The interview with Bill went exceptionally well, more like a conversation with an old friend rather than a tense exchange with a potential employer. At the end, they shook hands. Sonya appeared at the door. Bill instructed her to schedule Ethan for a drug and background check and to have him fill out his new hire paperwork while he was here.

"You can start as soon as the drug test and background check are completed. Welcome aboard, Ethan. I look forward to working with you," Bill congratulated him.

"Thanks, Mr. Jenkins. I'm very pleased to accept the position."

This was too good to be true. Ethan controlled himself long enough to make it to the parking lot, where he lifted the umbrella slightly higher and punched the air over his head with a fist of victory. He did not remember the ride over to Victoria's.

"I got the job," he announced as he entered the store.

"Don't tell me you're surprised," said Victoria.

"A bit. Part of me wanted to believe that the spell would work, but another part of me remained skeptical. I won't doubt again."

"You'll have no reason to," Victoria said.

"Thank you for working your magic on the situation. More good news. I found two local Witches that would like to meet you. When can we all get together?"

"They are unwilling participants, Ethan."

How did she know? Ethan thought. "Like I told them, let's just see how it goes."

Victoria's skepticism was apparent in her voice, "Dinner tomorrow at 7 pm. Another potential coven member is joining us as well. Heather Moorcroft."

"I'll let them know. See you then."

Victoria heard the bell ring as Ethan made his exit. "What do you think of him, Qadir?" she asked.

"He is a very young soul, but has potential to serve our purpose. If not, he's expendable like the others, and we will get ourselves another servant," Qadir responded from the shadows.

* * *

The heart came cleanly out of the man's chest, the vessels severed, sliced free by the ceremonial dagger. She held it out for all to see as though it were a newborn baby, careful not to allow the drippings to stain her purple satin robe. The blood glistened in the firelight. Anonymous faces cloaked in darkness stood silently witnessing the ancient ritual. Neither the crackling of burning wood nor the distant thunder had drowned out the man's last breath. That gurgling sound they make as they gasp for air through the blood in their throats. It happened every time, and she had grown to expect it.

Her ability to shape-shift was directly tied to the harvesting of fresh human hearts, which were getting increasingly difficult to come by. Her followers did the best they could, but it was risky work, performed with extreme caution. It was important to avoid headlines such as "Devil worshippers blamed for recent killings." The press loved that sort of thing; the readers gobbled it up; and the police, although skeptical, stepped up efforts to solve the crimes before the locals turned it into a witch-hunt. People started to suspect every teenager wearing a Nine Inch Nails tee shirt or a pentagram necklace.

What did they know? The devil had nothing to do with it. She wasn't even sure the devil existed. This practice was tied to an ancient ritual she found in a book about the Aztecs. They believed that human sacrifice was necessary to push the sun across the sky to prevent time from coming to an end. This had intrigued her, and she used the energy created by the Aztec's custom of cutting out the heart along with a spell derived from a 16th century book of Witchcraft. It proved to be a powerful combination, allowing her to transform herself into a large black cat. Her gray eyes would morph along with the rest of her, shaping her retina from round to feline slits. Cliché as it was, her body had naturally selected the shape of a cat the first time she had performed the ceremony. The spell lasted for five hours and was effective only at night.

Alexis munched popcorn and tried to remember the name of the film. Rainy afternoons were the perfect time to watch scary movies. The scene was far-fetched and over-dramatized in keeping with most horror films from the sixties. Her own ceremonies were peaceful and solitary. A Witch since birth, Alexis had performed various rituals and spells that were meant to help, not harm, others. She could make things happen. This talent taught her to be careful and to think about all the implications of even the most casual thought or wish.

The reason for her natural affinity for Witchcraft had become apparent yesterday morning in Macy's breakfast room. The amazing revelations that came through explained so much about the nature of her relationships with Macy and Cassandra and about the power they had as individuals. There had never been any doubt that Alexis had lived other lives in other times, yet no distinct memory of them had come through until now.

Prior to this, Alexis thought she had inherited her powers from her paternal grandmother in this life, Maria. Maria specialized in charms for protection and healing. Many people would come to the house seeking Maria's help. Little Alexis was tutored on the uses of herbs and minerals to create powerful talismans. Grandma taught Alexis the skill of energetic protection and the importance of positive intent when practicing The Craft. Alexis missed her grandmother. Alexis realized that Maria had been there to remind Alexis of who she is and to continue her ancient lessons.

Her movie ending with a predictable conclusion and the popcorn bowl empty, Alexis continued to ponder the situation. She needed to get over to the library, but she wanted to try something first. Her desire for more information prompted her to get the scrying mirror. It was round and black, the circumference edged in small silver droplets, creating a scalloped effect. She propped the mirror up on a stand so that it was at a 45-degree angle to her. This allowed her to comfortably peer into it from her chair. She arranged and lit candles on the table near the mirror: black for protection, white for blessings, and purple to encourage visions. Alexis lit a stick of sandalwood incense to complete the mystical atmosphere and promote protection.

She stood before the makeshift altar with a wand in hand, and pointed it toward the northeast. Turning clockwise, she forcefully announced, "I cast this circle to contain the energies I summon and to protect me from all that is unwelcome. I call the Watchers of the Four Directions and the God and Goddess to help me obtain information about my past life as a Witch and to protect me during my rite. Allow me to receive messages about this time with an open heart. Blessed be."

Having closed the circle, she felt safe in the energetic cocoon she had created. The candle flames danced at the corners of her vision and reflected off of the scrying mirror. She had conditioned herself to enter into a trance state under these conditions, prime for seeing and using her power of precognition. Smelling the familiar scent of sandalwood helped to banish her thoughts and give up control over the mundane images that entered her mind. Watching the thin line of smoke twist and wind itself around the candle flames was a form of self-induced hypnosis that she developed. Focusing on the floating spirals of smoke reacting to the slightest movement in the air or flick of the flame helped her to let go of all other thoughts.

She took several deep breaths, then relaxed her eyes and gazed at the mirror. It was the same every time: a fog would roll across her mind, and then a vague impression began to imprint itself onto the ether. Sometimes she would lose the image before it crystallized. Other times, it would come with such clarity that she no longer sat in her cozy Victorian dwelling, but would be wherever the vision took her.

The images would bring with them emotions that were partially her reactions to the vision and also feelings that were not her own, but rather attached to the image itself, as though one could not exist without the other. Several minutes passed before her physical vision clouded over and her mind's eye began to see with crystal clarity.

As Mina, my direction of power was the West. I was given the gifts of spirit contact and seeing into the future. My time of power was Twilight. Moon magic was my specialty. I had a teacher named Hala, who taught me wonderful things about herbs, just like Grandma. She also taught me of the power of gemstones. My abilities allowed me to see the future.

Alexis began to wonder about her teacher and allowed thoughts of how she missed her grandmother. The vision faded as Alexis longed to have a teacher once again. Hala, Maria, there had to be another waiting for her. The intimate sharing of knowledge and the accolades she received when she performed well were necessary components for Alexis to feel whole. She completed her ceremony by asking for a teacher to manifest in her life. Giving thanks, she removed the circle and released the Watchers and the God and Goddess from her service.

Mina always needed to feel close with people. She was sure that she had been emotionally attached to her teacher, Hala. In her life as Alexis, her parents died when she was 21. She missed her parents and believed that they were taken from her as part of a larger Universal plan. As the sole heir to their estate, she was left financially secure for life. Although her physical requirements were ensured, her emotional needs stood lacking. Macy and Cassandra were great friends and filled part of the void, but Alexis longed to be attached to a teacher once again.

A teacher would help her to avoid mistakes in spellcraft. Casting the wrong spell or doing it incorrectly could cause unwanted and potentially deadly situations. She recalled the day she purchased a book of spells and a special candle and was trying her hand at conjuring. She lit the candle and recited a spell for power. Then waited for a few minutes. Nothing seemed to be happening, so she went out. When she returned home, her key slid into the front door lock, turned the bolt smoothly from the jam, and the doorknob depressed easily; but the door would not open. She leaned her shoulder against the door and pushed hard. It felt as though someone was on the other side trying to keep it closed. The door opened under duress. As she entered the foyer, the air was dense with supernatural activity. Many entities were present and swirling about. She stepped inside and closed the door behind her.

Alexis blamed the spell she had chanted for the ghostly turmoil. She retrieved the book from the cocktail table, a white candle, a small vial with a lid, and a Bible. The white candle and Bible were blessed to turn them into powerful tools against the eerie onslaught. The vial was for holy water from the church reservoir. On her way to the church, she threw the book of spells into a dumpster at the gas station down the street.

When she returned home, she lit the white candle and read aloud Psalm 91, God's protection, while burning sandalwood and sage to help cleanse the negative entities from the house. After about thirty minutes, the air felt lighter and the activity lessened. There were only a few ethereal visitors remaining and she guided them to the light. By morning, the house was clear. Alexis later learned that she had opened the gate but had not closed it after the spell was cast, allowing multitudes of unwanted entities into her house. She had not cast a circle of containment and protection. While she was able to overcome the blunder, avoiding it would be better. The incident of uncontrolled spirits showed her how much trouble she could get into without the right guidance. A teacher was necessary until she could recall her lessons from her ancient incarnation.

Alexis had not experienced her past life gift of precognition, but since the spell-gone-awry incident, she could see spirits. Just as her parents' death was out of her control, so were the visions of entities that would stand at the edge of her peripheral vision. She saw both men and women, moving and standing still, outside and inside. Sometimes the being was a small animal, dark and hairy, sitting or standing near her. Alexis would catch glimpses of these presences frequently, their appearances apparently not tied to anything. She could not find a pattern. At times, they just stood watching her from a doorway and at other times, they were going about their business, walking around and paying no attention whatsoever to Alexis. She was used to their presence and so was rarely disturbed by them.

Alexis snuffed out the candles and returned the scrying mirror to its protective case. She was tired but promised the others she would go to the library before they got together for dinner that evening. She climbed the steps, appreciating the details of her house: the ornamental banister of dark carved oak, the thick crown molding, and the fireplace in the bedroom. It was part of her inheritance and allowed her to keep strong memories of her parents with her. She dressed in jeans and a short-sleeved sweater and, grabbing an umbrella, headed out to the library.

It was a short walk from her house, down Main Street to West Ferry. To take the car was more trouble than it was worth. Parking was difficult and the lots were just as far from the library as her house was. Even with the light rain, she enjoyed being outside. The rain cooled the air and provided a soothing backdrop to her thoughts. The information desk was not far from the entrance. Alexis approached the desk and she shook off her umbrella.

"May I help you?" a pleasant, dark-haired woman inquired.

Alexis saw her nametag: Maxine Ashcraft. "Yes, please, Maxine. My name is Alexis. I'm looking for the ancient history section. More specifically, information on the Great Library of Alexandria."

"One of my favorites!" exclaimed Maxine. "I'd be happy to help you with that. Follow me."

Alexis followed Maxine through the maze of tall bookcases. She always loved libraries: the smell of books and the hush they demanded.

"You know they are rebuilding the Great Library," Maxine offered.

"No, I didn't. I was hoping to get information about the ancient structure and what it contained."

"It was a place like no other; a vessel for an estimated 700,000 scrolls containing the knowledge of the known world. Bibliotheca Alexandrina became the center of learning, becoming the world's first university." Maxine sighed. Alexis thought she saw tears in her eyes as she continued. "The library was gradually destroyed from the time of Caesar's invasion, including a fire that ravaged Alexandria. The final straw came in 391 A.D. when Theodosius I ordered all pagan temples and other structures razed. It was a great loss."

"You speak of it as though you were there," teased Alexis.

"I read a lot and the books transport me to the places they speak of. Being a librarian, it hurts me to think of ancient writings being burned and lost to humanity forever." Maxine explained. "I have often fantasized about the Great Library and what it was like to study there."

"Have you come across anything that told about some very special scrolls? Ones that held a great deal of power?"

"Knowledge is power. Stories about magic scrolls are greatly embellished," said Maxine. "There is a text you may be interested in that holds esoteric significance and supposedly has power over good and evil." She pulled a volume down from the shelf.

The leather-bound book was thin with the title embossed across the front and gold-edged pages. Alexis silently read the title – *The Seven Evil Spirits*; then turned to the opening page, which read: *R.C. Thompson, translator [The Devils and Evil Spirits of Babylonia,*

London 1903].[1]. The second part of the book contained a charm against the seven evil spirits and the text of the Seven Fires and Seven Thunders.

"These are very ancient legends taken from the sixteenth tablet of a series called the 'Evil Demon Series', its origin residing in Assyria," said Maxine.

"I'll take this one. I need to get going, but if you come across anything else you think would help me, please put it aside, and I'll be back tomorrow. I really appreciate all of the information you've given me," said Alexis.

"It's what I do," Maxine smiled. "I'll keep digging. See you tomorrow."

Maxine checked out the book to Alexis and watched her walk toward the door into the rainy twilight. She hoped that Alexis would begin to remember the ancient past on her own sooner than later and planned to help spark the memory with some choice reading material.

⚞ 6 ⚟

Heather arrived at Victoria's home promptly at 7 pm, during a break in the weather, dressed in her best pair of conservative tan slacks and a tweed blazer she bought during her last attempt at shopping five years before. Sales people seemed repelled by her, so Heather did not enjoy the shopping experience. Stores were another place where she was among people, yet felt totally alone, so she repeatedly wore what was already in her closet. Heather worked from home as a virtual customer service agent for an insurance company, so there was no need to buy clothes for the office. The job gave her a steady income, albeit small, and the ability to be in contact with people without physically being in their presence.

When Victoria invited her to join them for dinner, Heather was overwhelmed with gratitude. Heather wanted so much to belong. She wondered why Victoria had extended the invitation, since most could not tolerate her presence for more than a few minutes, let alone schedule an extended visit. Although curious, it did not matter why Victoria had asked her to join them. It would be good to spend some time with people.

Victoria welcomed her into her home and offered her a glass of Merlot, as Heather handed her the tiramisu she brought as a gift. Heather accepted the drink, hoping it would relax her. Heather had not been around people in so long, she was unsure how to behave. Victoria waved her to sit on the antique sofa in the living room. Heather gazed up at the thick crown molding and cranberry-colored walls. She sat on the tapestry cushions of the sofa and took a sip of wine. A knock on the door prompted Victoria to vanish for a moment and return with a handsome young man and two odd-looking women. Heather hoped her lack of confidence would not be apparent to them.

"Ethan Talbot, meet Heather Moorcroft," said Victoria.

He smiled and extended his hand to her. "Victoria told me she had invited you to join us this evening. We're glad to have you here and hope that you'll decide to become part of the group. Let me introduce two other potential group members, Sandy and Helen."

They greeted Victoria, handing her a small bouquet of flowers and a bottle of wine; then acknowledged Heather.

Heather wondered if either of the women was Ethan's girlfriend and if he was attracted to the black lace and odd jewelry that adorned them. She had a deep desire to be part of a group, although she was unsure of what the group was about. She felt compelled to find out. Heather was drawn to Victoria and Ethan in a way she had never before experienced, although she was not yet sure about Sandy and Helen. She noticed that none of them was fatigued or bothered by her presence, and that drew her closer to them without fear of rejection. Her inability to pull on their energy fields or drink from their essence gave rise to her hopes that she could remain with them. She felt safe in their presence.

Everyone was seated and held a glass of wine.

"Is everyone here a member of the group?" Heather asked.

"Not yet," said Victoria.

"How many members are there?" wondered Heather.

"Five, if everyone here decides to join, one for each point on the pentagram," said Victoria.

"What kind of group is it?" inquired Heather, curious to know what kind of group would have only five members.

"It is a very exclusive group, one in which you must have special gifts to join," said Victoria.

"What special gifts do you think I have that allows me to be here with you now?" asked Heather, confused at what they saw in her. No one had ever singled her out as having a talent or trait that was useful or distinctive.

Victoria smiled. "You have the gift of using your mind and body energies to manipulate the life energy of others. Right now, all you can do is pull energy from others, to feed yourself. We can teach you to use your natural ability very effectively and to control it so that others can comfortably be in your presence."

How did they know? wondered Heather. *Who are these people?*

"We are your new teachers, if you'll have us," Victoria answered her thoughts.

Heather looked at her, startled.

Sandy and Helen listened and looked at each other.

"We comprise what is formally known as a coven. Our work in the magical arts is diverse and extends to both the light and the dark side of things," clarified Victoria.

Heather took a larger pull from the wine glass. "Do you mean to tell me that you're Witches?

"To put it bluntly, yes," Ethan answered, amused by her realization. "Sandy and Helen have been practicing Witches for..."

"As long as we can remember," answered Helen. She gazed at Victoria.

Another gulp of wine, and Victoria was next to her refilling the glass. She was feeling lightheaded and confused. Should it matter to her that they practiced their magic on the dark side of things? All of the stories about witches she had ever heard said they were evil and cautioned to steer clear of associations with them. Yet, of all the people she had ever encountered in her life, these were the only ones who welcomed her. They provided the acceptance and companionship that she had been searching for all of her life. Now, in her mid-thirties, she had found a home where her spirit was not judged and her appetite for the life force of others was not admonished.

"I'm nervous and excited about what you are telling me. I accept your offer and am grateful that you have chosen me to be part of such a limited group. I'll do my best to learn what you feel I should know and to make you proud," decided Heather with a smile. She raised her wine glass in salute to them both.

"Outstanding," applauded Ethan.

Victoria smiled her approval. By recruiting Heather Moorcroft, Victoria was hoping to accomplish two goals. The first was for Ethan to direct his self-proclaimed charm on Heather rather than Victoria. A minor makeover would transform Heather into a source of attraction rather than the drab presentation sitting before her. The second was to develop Heather's natural gift as a psi-vampire. Heather came to Victoria with a high degree of natural ability to drain the energy of others. Starved for affection, she would willingly accept Ethan's advances. Ethan and Heather could play together if they wished, until Victoria needed Heather to use her gift.

"How about you two? Are you feeling the vibe?" Ethan asked.

Sandy and Helen looked at each other. "We are still considering the offer. We've been solitary practitioners for a long time," said Sandy.

"Who was your teacher?" asked Victoria.

"We are self-taught. Our knowledge has come through intuition and practice," replied Helen.

Victoria was unsettled at her inability to read these women. They were cloaked in a solid wall of energy that she could not penetrate. It was quite impressive for ones who taught themselves The Craft.

"I'd like to hear more about your philosophy as it pertains to the practice of Witchcraft," Sandy said to Victoria.

"How about telling them over dinner? I'm starving!" Ethan demanded.

They sat at the dining room table while Victoria brought out the salmon, asparagus, and a large green salad. She noticed that Sandy and Helen ate the vegetables but avoided the fish.

"Vegetarians?" ask Victoria.

"Yes, for many years," said Helen.

Heather took a chance and asked, "Why?"

"It keeps our energy clear and light so that we are able to direct it more efficiently. Animal protein has a heavier vibration than vegetable matter. While fish and other seafood tend to be of a lighter vibration than mammals, we have chosen to avoid it on general principal. We don't eat anything that has a consciousness," answered Sandy.

"I thought that there has been research where plants respond to fire and other negative stimuli. Doesn't that mean they are conscious?" asked Ethan.

"Plants have a life force fueled by The Source of All That Is; yet to say they are consciously aware is a stretch. Trees have the strongest auric fields. Asparagus not as much," Sandy said as she popped the tip of a spear in her mouth. "So Victoria, tell us about what your coven's intention will be."

Victoria's eyes narrowed at the wording of the question. "The intention depends upon the circumstances."

"You mentioned the practice of both light and dark arts. Can you expand on that concept?" pushed Helen.

"Balance is important. The type of conjuration depends on the situation at hand. To practice only white magic is to negate the existence of the dark. We must stay aware and adept at the practice of both in order to be able to defend ourselves and to accomplish our purpose."

"And our purpose is..." Sandy sought to clarify Victoria's vague explanation.

"To raise awareness of ourselves and the vibration of the planet, of course." Victoria smiled.

"Of course," agreed Sandy, with a touch of sarcasm.

"So the purpose of the group is to know ourselves and each other better?" Heather asked, hoping that she understood.

"The power of The Craft comes from self-knowledge, so that will certainly be a primary goal," said Victoria.

"The development of will is essential to the successful practice of magic. At the same time, it is imperative to tap into the Divine will, not just that of the self," explained Sandy.

"Caution is to be used when pursuing the dark side of The Craft and of the self. The Rule of Three always applies," Helen said to Heather.

"The Rule of Three?" Ethan wanted to understand as well.

"Whatever you do, whatever energy you send out, comes back to you threefold. If you choose to cast a negative spell toward someone, expect the energy of that act to come back to you three times as strong. The same applies to positive acts or spells. The goodness is blessed upon you three times over your one," said Sandy.

"You girls are certainly well-versed in Universal Law. Your understanding of the ethics and responsibility of what we do is commendable. You would be powerful additions to the coven," said Victoria, still wary of what these two were capable of.

"We will ask for guidance and come to you with a decision by the end of the week, said Helen. Sandy nodded in agreement.

"Fair enough," said Ethan. "I'm ready for the tiramisu Heather brought." Ethan flashed his best smile at Heather, and she felt herself flush.

Victoria said nothing as she got up to get dessert plates.

* * *

Sandy and Helen said goodnight and left Ethan at Victoria's. They walked in silence for two blocks before feeling it was safe to talk.

"Do you think it's her?" Sandy asked.

"I couldn't get a read on her, but I did feel a funky energy coming from the basement" said Helen.

Even two floors removed, the women had felt the powerful energy emanating from the subterranean section of the building.

"It's uncomfortable to be around her. It reminds me of being around Qadir in the old days," said Sandy with a shiver.

"The only way to know what she's up to may be to join the coven. At the same time, it may be risky. She knows we aren't the run-of-the-mill Wicca practitioners from Upper Bucks County. She hasn't recognized us, either. I can tell by the way she was reacting to us," Helen thought aloud.

"And of course, Ethan is clueless. We need to locate Iman and Uzma and try to awaken them. The web of Amira's spell of forgetting is coming apart. I want to be there when they start to remember," rationalized Helen.

"Won't they be surprised to see us," Sandy mused.

Teaming up with the virtuous members of the Triad Witches was the only way for Sandy and Helen to recover the scrolls. Victoria's deception as Amira was an abuse of the knowledge and power she acquired through her studies. The spell against the Triad Witches locked the protective vessel that contained the scrolls. Not until the others awaken could the box be opened. Amira had been chastising herself for centuries for not understanding how the power worked. The scrolls were inaccessible all this time. Amira was coming closer to tapping into the power she had waited so long to control.

* * *

With Ethan and Heather gone, Victoria decided to visit the vault. The basement not only held items for the store, but it had a bonus feature as well. A small room accessible by a three-by-three foot opening in the cinderblock wall behind the heater had closed the sale on the property. Victoria discovered it when the realtor went outside to have a smoke. Once through the small opening, she was able to stand comfortably inside. There were no windows for prying eyes, and the opening was easily concealed. This is where special treasures were stored, primeval treasures that were much work to move and hide.

She descended the narrow staircase and pulled the chain to the single bulb hanging from the ceiling. A 60-watt bulb lit the center of the room, but left shadows in the corners. The board behind the heater could not be readily seen. Victoria slid it to the side and squatted down to maneuver into the hidden space. She flicked a lighter and lit several candles standing on small tables that lined the walls of the room. A soft glow reflected from the silver casing and lapis lazuli gemstones that adorned the primordial vessel. How she wished she could open the box to gaze upon her longed-for treasures. Amira had waited lifetimes.

It had been centuries since it all began, and yet it seemed like only yesterday that she betrayed her coven and wiped their memories clean. Her treachery was devastating, and she regretted it almost immediately, so she cast a spell designed to prevent them from remembering. There were times when she regretted the action that separated her from her original coven so deeply, that she shut herself away, unable to function. The power that she stole was potent in its own right, but it had been a lonely road. Victoria's attempts to create a powerful coven to replace them were unsuccessful. No combination of witches since had the strength that the Triad Witches enjoyed together. She remembered their childhood together with fondness.

They were sorceresses raised and trained to channel their powers and direct them in very specific ways. In the protected environment provided by the High Priests and Priestesses, they thrived. All daily activities were done as a group, with their teachers watching over them. The four of them were constant companions, loving to experiment with their powers even during playtime. The deep friendship that existed among them increased their ability to perform as a team. They became known as the Triad Witches, for they knew the secrets of combining the mind, body, and spirit to manifest their desires.

The four of them represented each direction and each element: Uzma was South and Fire; Iman was East and Air; Mina was West and Water; and Amira was North and Earth. Their union unleashed the elemental powers to their maximum potential. Victoria's body shivered as she remembered the electrifying feeling that came from performing their rituals. Many in the ancient world heard of them and reacted with reverence or with fear. People came from afar to consult with the Triad Witches on important decisions and eventualities. The majority came seeking advice and counsel. There were others who believed that they had become too powerful and attempted to terminate their existence. Those who came with negative intent were revealed and their motivation extinguished before they could reach the gate of the Temple's walled compound.

Victoria considered the situation. It would be difficult, if not impossible, to overcome them, should they reunite. They are a powerful force to reckon with. Individually they possess abilities beyond that of the average Witch. Together, there is nothing they could not accomplish, even without a fourth. The beam that emanated from them when they gathered was blinding white at its fullest. Amira hoped that the truth would never be revealed. She wanted ultimate power, but vowed never to harm her three sisters unless it became absolutely necessary.

The Watchers had helped them find each other in every lifetime, waiting for the Witches to recall their power and their purpose. Their names and faces changed with each incarnation, so it was a chore to locate them with each new life. So far her magic had ensured that their memories had not returned. Yet, many centuries have passed, and the binding spell was beginning to lose its threads. She had not anticipated that sealing their memories would seal the sacred vessel as well.

With each rebirth, she retained the knowledge and abilities she developed during her training in ancient Mesopotamia, and her power had grown with each incarnation. The many identities Amira had taken in the lifetimes since then tested her patience. She found it cumbersome to go through childhood again and again. Being under someone else's control and guidance, unable to exercise her volition, was a tedious affair. She was always viewed as "different" from her family and from other children in the neighborhood. As she aged, her abilities reemerged, and her strength slowly built until she fully regained her powers. But her destiny evaded her, and the scrolls lay hidden and useless. As the others began to remember, the scrolls would once again be available to achieve her desires.

Amira's attempts to control the scrolls in ancient times were unsuccessful. Legend said that they could be used to bring about chaos and disaster throughout the world. Her intent was not to destroy civilization, but rather to rule and control others. For the most part, she enjoyed the world as it was, and as it is. Only those who are inferior would suffer under her rule. She stood in the candlelight fantasizing about her first act as Supreme Goddess.

"And you will do *my* bidding, Amira," whispered Qadir from a dark corner of the room, shaking Victoria from her thoughts.

"Qadir, am I to have no privacy at all?"

"You would not be here now if I hadn't taught you to how to remember in each lifetime. I demand gratitude," his anger lying just below his controlled tone.

"Forgive me. All will be as you wish," Victoria sighed, a tear glistening in the corner of her eye.

* * *

Alexis and Cassandra arrived at the same time. They hugged in Macy's driveway and together walked to the front door. All three women were excited to learn more about the scrolls and the role they played. Over dinner, Alexis shared the information she had gleaned from Maxine. Macy went into more detail about the prayer ritual she had witnessed during her trance session with the censer.

"But what do we do with this information now that we have it?" asked Alexis. "It's all fascinating, but why are we able to know these things now?"

"Maybe we weren't ready before," interpreted Cassandra. "Information does not come through until you're ready to hear it."

"I wonder what Victoria's game is," pondered Macy. "She must know that I can pick up energy and images from objects. Which then makes me question why she would put the incense burner in my path?"

"Does she want us to remember?" asked Alex.

"It's hard to say," said Macy. "Let's try to understand more about the scrolls. Maybe that will give us a clue."

"Tonight I brought Runes," said Cassandra. "This set is made of Amethyst and will be a powerful tool to provide messages. The Amethyst opens the third eye and enhances psychic awareness. The symbols etched in the stones will indicate the messages we are to receive. We'll go around the table, each asking a question, and pulling Rune stones from the bag. Start your question with the phrase 'Give me a message about...' I'll go first."

Cassandra put her whole hand in the bag and held all of the Runes in her palm. She said, "Give me a message about the scrolls from ancient times." She let the stones fall between her fingers until a few remained in her palm. These she pulled from the bag and positioned them carefully on the table. There were four Runes waiting for interpretation.

"There were four scrolls, each containing an elemental force and indicating a direction. The first Rune is Laguz, which is the Rune for Flow. It represents the element of Water and so one scroll is associated with the West. Antares was the Watcher of the West and in control of the Autumnal Equinox. Within the Scroll of the West Wind was held all aspects of positive intent, kindness, goodness, compassion, and wisdom.

"The second Rune is Thurisaz or Gateway. It carries with it the element of Air, so is the scroll of the East. This scroll contained the energy of the Divine. The Watcher of the East, Aldebaran, also ruled the Vernal Equinox.

"The next Rune is called Algiz. It is the Rune of protection. From the fire of the South, the world is protected by the Mystery of the Seven Fires and was the only antidote to the evil that emanated from its companion, the scroll of the North, which held the Secret of the Seven Evil Spirits that lay in wait to unleash their storm of decimation upon the earth. Hagalaz, the Rune of Disruption, represents the scroll of the North. The Watcher in the South was Regulus, guarding the vibration of the Summer Solstice. The Watcher of the North was called Fomalhaut, who stood over the Winter Solstice. "

"Which reminds me about the biggest find from the library." Alexis pulled out the leather bound text and handed it to Macy. The others gasped. "Talk about dead on, Cassandra!" Alexis admired Cassandra's ability to pull information.

"I'll say," said Macy. "These texts were whispered to me in my vision. Somehow I was taught about them as part of my responsibility in ancient times."

"It may also be part of your responsibility in the present," corrected Cassandra.

"By the way, how do you know about The Watchers?" asked Alexis. "There are Watchers in Stregheria, the Italian form of Witchcraft, but where did you get such details?"

"It came through. I never heard of them before. We must be tapping into something very powerful for them to be communicating so directly."

The Runes were placed back in the bag. It was Macy's turn to pull.

"Give me a message as to why there are four scrolls."

Two Runes clung to her palm. Macy pulled them out of the bag and placed them gently on the table. They were Sowelu, the Rune of Wholeness, and Gebo, the Rune of Partnership.

Cassandra began her interpretation. "The Watchers decreed that all four must exist in order to maintain energetic stability in the universe. Keeping the four texts in close proximity of each other ensures the essential balance that prevents celestial calamity."

Alexis felt her mind whirling, eager to get more information. "I'm going to ask Maxine about the Watchers. There must be something she can dig up in the library about this."

Cassandra slid the bag over to Alexis. She reached in and pulled one Rune from the bag.

"Teiwaz," said Cassandra, "The Warrior Rune. Looks like we are about to enter into battle, ladies, and we must prepare."

≈ 7 ≈

The rain continued, and Alexis walked to the library, stepping over puddles and twirling her umbrella above her. The warm, damp air accompanied Alexis on her journey. Maxine was waiting for her at the front desk, excited to see her come in.

"I found it!" she exclaimed.

"Tell me!"

"The legend of the Scrolls of the Four Winds. It was in a volume of archaic myths. It's a reference book that can't be checked out of the library, so I photocopied the page for you." Maxine handed it to Alexis.

Her eyes widened as she read.

The planets were aligned to produce a most miraculous coming, as was foretold by the Ancients. The citizens of Ur rejoiced, knowing that the prophecy had come to pass. The infants possessed spiritual gifts the likes of which the Elders had never seen. They were born into this world for the sole purpose of shielding the Scrolls of the Four Winds from misuse. Their parents had been carefully chosen from among the most gifted and scholarly members of the Temple of the Moon God Nanna Sin. Four females, representing each of the four directions, had come into being at four different times of power on this day.

If they failed and the scrolls fell into the wrong hands, they could be used to bring about chaos and disaster throughout the world.

The scrolls themselves could not be destroyed, for they were created by the pure consciousness and powerful intent of the Watchers, whose stellar energies held unlimited power, perfect knowledge, and clear vision. These light beings made the scrolls as a gift to humankind in an attempt to exemplify the need for balance and harmony between all entities, living and non-living, those with consciousness and those without. The sacred texts held the balance of the known world; their existence was crucial to sustain the matrix of vitality, which allows energy to be moved and directed. Under benevolent eyes of those charged with their keeping, humans would experience clarity and understanding, the ability to see beyond themselves into the energies that connect all living things. Under an egocentric guardian, the scrolls would reveal the shadow side of humanity—prejudice, hatred, and war.

The manuscripts were blessed under the light of the full moon as the scrolls descended from the Heavens on the last leg of their journey to Earth. Absorbing the radiant magic of the celestial satellite allowed absolute power to imbed itself into their pages. The scrolls contained the energy of the elemental forces of Earth (North Wind), Air (East Wind), Fire (South Wind), and Water (West Wind). The Watcher of the East, Aldebaran, also ruled the Vernal Equinox. In the South was Regulus, guarding the vibration of the Summer Solstice. Antares was in the West and in control of the Autumnal Equinox. The Watcher of the North was called Fomalhaut, who stood over the Winter Solstice. Within the Scroll of the West Wind was held all aspects of positive intent, kindness, goodness, and compassion. The Scroll of the South Wind held the Mystery of the Seven Fires and was the only antidote to the evil that emanated from its companion, the Scroll of the North Wind, which held the Secret of the Seven Evil Spirits that lay in wait to unleash their storm of decimation upon the earth. The Scroll of the East Wind carried the energy of the Divine. The light that radiated from it was gold and white. The Watchers decreed that all four must exist in order to maintain energetic stability. Keeping the four texts in close proximity of each other ensured the essential balance that prevented calamity.

"My God!" Alexis cried. "Thank you so much, Maxine!"

Before Maxine could reply, Alexis was out the door.

Maxine thought of Alexis as she processed the books of the next library patron. Would she come back to the library now that she had the information she was looking for? Just in case, Maxine had her home address in phone number on her library profile. Things could get sticky, and Alexis was on the verge of awakening. She had some pertinent information, but did not remember her heritage fully. Centuries had passed since Maxine was Hala, teacher of Alexis known as Mina in ancient Mesopotamia. Hala knew Mina's full power and needed to reunite with her. She could feel Amira close by, waiting to sink her claws into Hala's student.

* * *

Victoria watched with an astral eye as Alexis and Maxine exchange information. Could that be Hala, Alexis's ancient teacher? She is one who knew the history of the Watchers and of the Scrolls of the Four

Winds. Victoria knew she had to be certain of Hala's identity before the others discovered her whereabouts.

The bell on the shop door tinkled, set to motion as a customer entered the store. Victoria reluctantly pulled back from her astral journey, watching the image of the women flicker and fade the closer her etheric double came to her physical body. Her ability to astral project came in handy when there was a need to listen undetected. Using the astral body is a unique mode of traveling. There is always an element of uncertainty when your body separates from its spirit, tethered only by a thin silver cord. She occasionally liked to test the maximum length of the cord, wondering at what point it would snap, rendering her permanently detached from her body. Although she was adept at transformational magic, she felt the need to exercise her astral body every so often. She let the customer know she was available to answer any questions about the items. Victoria could tell this woman was only browsing.

Victoria remembered the day she met the mysterious Columbian man who taught her this valuable skill. He had come into the shop looking for a print of Waterhouse's "Circe, Invidiosa." Circe was a witch in ancient times, blamed for using herbs and incantations to turn Odysseus's men into swine. Being a witch herself, she had procured many items with attachment to The Craft and so had a copy of it, handsomely framed in a heavily carved gilded molding. As she wrote up the cash sale, a conversation ensued about Circe's powers. Circe could hide the moon or the sun behind clouds, and destroy her enemies with poisonous potions. In her presence, the woods could move, the ground rumble, and the trees around her turn white.

The gentleman commented that while Circe could perform these feats, she did not pursue the ability to astral project. If she had, there would have been no need to wait for wayward sailors to arrive at her island. She could have gone to them. If the ability to astral project could be honed to such an expert degree, it would be possible to travel anywhere at will in the spirit body. Victoria was fascinated by the concept and asked for a demonstration. He agreed to visit her in his astral body that evening, but would not say a specific time. The experiment would be compromised if too much information were given. She agreed to the challenge. He left the shop, never revealing his name.

That evening, Victoria grew tired of waiting for the arrival of the gentleman's astral body and went to bed. Sleep was invaded by vivid images of white light and a gateway in the traditional dimensions. Concepts of time and space were obliterated by these visions. As she watched, a man stepped through the opening. It was the Columbian gentleman, his black hair slicked back at the top and ending in a cascade of long waves, smiling and holding out his hand. His palm was facing upward and a glow, like fire without heat, could be seen in the center of it. He stood next to her bed in this position for several minutes before she awoke and looked to see if he was physically standing there. So realistic was the vision that she wondered how he had known where she lived and how he had gotten into the house. Shaken, Victoria was unable to drift back to sleep.

The following day, the man returned to her shop. He mentioned nothing about what had transpired the previous evening. Talking casually about the painting he had purchased and how grand it looked in his home, Victoria could feel his anticipation. Unable to wait any longer, Victoria shared the vision of her dream. Smiling slyly as he had the night before, he revealed that what she saw as a flame in his palm was a crystal pyramid that he had been holding out to her. Because Victoria was able to pick up the vision, he rewarded her by sharing his name—Julian Gaviria.

Victoria's mind was on fire considering all the potential uses of this skill. There would be no limit to where she could impose herself. She could spy on those she mistrusted; get pertinent information from and instill fear in her enemies. Victoria vowed to become a student of astral projection. Julian schooled her over a 14-month period.

"What if you're not able to return to your body?" Victoria inquired.

"The first time I had trouble returning, it frightened me into a panic. The only thing I could think to do was to say a prayer I had learned as a child in Columbia. I said it over and over and over until I was pulled back into my body. Panic is what prevents the return," he said.

This was the first lesson he taught her. The second lesson was never to perform astral projection, scrying, evocations, or consecrations during the Tempus eversionis, the time between the Winter Solstice and the Vernal Equinox. This is the dark tide of the seasons, a time of withdrawal meant for works that take the sorceress within, such as meditation and cleansing to prepare for the renewal that comes in the spring. Julian had taught her well.

Victoria remembered that in all of her astral journeys, reminding herself not to panic, and arming herself with a familiar set of words that would calm her. She chose prayers taught to her by her ancient teacher, Qadir. His legendary knowledge of demons and the Seven Evil Spirits was essential in preparing her to develop a deep understanding of the dark powers, her allies. Under Qadir's tutelage, she aligned herself with the energy held within the shadows and used her abilities to defend against the dark forces. Victoria's talent for invoking spirits to do her bidding quickly became apparent under Qadir's guidance. The Elders knew that this type of lesson had a certain level of risk to it and prayed that the influence of the other children would temper the possibility that she would move onto the dark path. Qadir had become withdrawn over the years, and his allegiance was suspect, yet he had achieved the highest level of knowledge on the subjects necessary for Victoria to fulfill her role. The Elders watched him closely as he taught her The Craft.

It became easy to command spirits under Qadir's guidance. She was able to do it still. It had been fun to send the hoard of spirits to Alexis's house, making her think she had conjured them. Now that she had listened to Alexis and the others, their strength grew. She had heard enough to know that they came closer to the truth, searching using their innate abilities to scan the past. Victoria knew they were aware of her identity, as well as becoming more aware of their own, despite her attempts at cloaking herself from recognition.

She could have chosen to cast another spell on them, but decided that hiding herself energetically took less energy than stopping the three of them from seeing. It was a drain on her nonetheless. Surrounded in darkness each time they came together while simultaneously keeping an astral eye on them was challenging. Sharing the memories of their combined pasts made her think about the scrolls and of their hiding place.

Victoria's eavesdropping forced her to relive the primordial memory with Macy and the others and felt a longing for the group to reunite. Although Victoria was fearful of having the coven remember their history, to cast the same spell as she did centuries ago would be detrimental to their energetic health. Victoria was surprised that after all this time and preparation, her desire for solitary power was waning. With these memories, she recalled the extraordinary power they felt together. Would they accept her once they remembered? She was willing to give up the power she took, even though she had planned on more time to try to harness it for her personal goals. She wondered if they would be able to control the power of the scrolls together.

But her dark side, the part of her she fought to suppress since childhood, bubbled up now and then, and resented that recognition was tied to the group instead of her individual assets. She felt that her own talents far exceeded the others. They held her back from achieving singular notoriety. As Amira her private time was spent exerting her magical skills upon the staff of the temple, forcing them to do her bidding through mere force of will. She practiced the dark arts, including spells that would negatively affect the mind and physical body of her target. Qadir taught these incantations to her after he had been denied the opportunity to become a high priest of the temple because of his wicked tendencies.

Victoria remembered thinking that the other three Witches seemed so content. They were void of ambition and limited in their vision compared to the fantasies of power that swirled in her mind. Victoria's rule over the dark spirits was insufficient to quench her thirst for control over others. To enchant the known world with her spells and have all at her command, from royalty down to the lowliest servant, was Victoria's dream and a promise to herself. She planned to use the others as a vehicle to fulfill her desires. Being a part of this coven brought prestige and entrance to sanctuaries that would have otherwise been deemed off-limits. As a Triad Witch, entrusted to secure the great texts, she was granted entrance to the secret vault where The Scrolls of the Four Winds were hidden. And secure them she had. She thought that to possess them would complete her power and enable her to rule uncontested. There would be no equal to her domination. Her magic would prevail and subdue all those who would oppose her. This fantasy always made her smile and helped to grow the beam of light they conjured as a group.

Oh the desires of youth, daydreams without boundary! The combination of youth and inexperience had not dissuaded her wishes. She did not know the extent of the power she selfishly sought to possess. There are some things that cannot be controlled. Not even the most powerful Witch can play the role of Supreme Being.

So as not to bear the entire burden, Victoria enlisted the help of her current coven. They showed promise toward the nocturnal practice of The Craft, but lacked discipline and focus. They relied on Victoria, their High Priestess, to learn Witchcraft. In the process, they would learn about themselves, for the ability to perform magic and knowledge of oneself are inseparable. Victoria assigned Ethan Talbot to keep an eye on Macy once he begins his new job. It would be easy for him to observe her at the office. As he watches her, Victoria would watch him. She was aware that Ethan was self-serving, egotistical, and pretended to be one with the goals of the coven. While annoying, he served Victoria's purposes—for now. He honestly believed that Victoria could not see his true motivations. No problem, for there were benefits to being underestimated.

When Victoria assigned him to spy on Macy, she did not tell him why. She knew better than to confide in Ethan and was careful to limit what she taught him regarding the occult arts. After the lesson in mind reading, he took the risk of trying to read Victoria directly. Of course she felt it and retaliated by blasting him with jolt of blinding energy. It would take him many lifetimes to master good judgment. He reveals himself at every turn, yet does not have the ability to observe his errors. The danger this created was incalculable; Victoria was careful to feed him only crumbs of information rather than giving him the big picture. He was tired of the veil of secrecy that surrounded important matters and felt that he should be named High Priest of the Coven of Dark Mysteries and be given equal control. Not likely, thought Victoria.

* * *

The Southeastern Pennsylvania Transportation Authority regional rail seemed to move more slowly on rainy days. Using public transportation felt like stepping into an open wound. Each person boarding the train was encapsulated in their own shell, making conscious effort to avoid mixing their energies with the energies of those around them. Some riders were so successful at separating themselves that they did not know (or care) that they were elbowing the person sitting next to them. Ignoring each other, yet responding with a group mentality when the lights on the train dimmed, or when the smell of burning breaks floated into the car, the passengers took their isolated journeys.

Some of the regulars formed small groups, creating friendships that lasted from where they had boarded to their final destination. No phone numbers were exchanged, no sense of history passed between them, and yet there was a sense of the present and the drama that ran through their lives. One or two incidences would be shared and followed-up on. If a regular was not on the train, the others wondered if he or she was all right. Speculations would ensue, getting the real story upon the absent member's return.

Macy was as guilty as the rest as far as isolating herself, and only built the commuter friendships that were based on the rigors of the commute itself. Sometimes Macy allowed her third eye to open on the train. During one trip, a young Asian woman sitting next to her was reading an article about applying for a fellowship grant in physics. Macy knew that this woman would not get the fellowship and was not intellectually capable of competing in her chosen field. Disappointed, Macy went back to reading her book.

Another time, one of the regulars, Eric, a middle-aged father of one, was sharing a story about his wife's desire to put their eight-year-old daughter into an all-girl school. A debate ensued, with Macy expressing concern that the girl would not be adequately socialized to compete in a male-dominated business world. That without exposure to brothers, or males of any sort other than her father, she would lack understanding as to how males think and interact. As she was saying this, Macy suddenly knew that the young woman standing to her right was an only child and had attended an all-girl school. Macy looked at the woman, who, without saying anything to Macy, confirmed that she went to an all-girl school, had no brothers, and turned out just fine. The lesson to remember was to open her third eye first, rather than her mouth.

Macy's ride to Philadelphia from New Hope each day gave her time to plan her day, read, or just get in some down time. The passengers sat quietly on the 6:17 am train leaving from Yardley. It was too early in the morning to strike up a conversation. Some worked on laptop computers. Some slept. Macy looked out the rain-spattered window as they passed mature maples, sycamores, and pine trees. The air felt warm but not stifling this morning, summer's humidity was dissipating.

It was a couple of weeks until autumn, her most powerful from a psychic perspective, and her mind readily pulled information from people and objects. Impressions from the woman sitting next to her included an argument she had had with her husband this morning and worrying about a meeting with her boss. Macy received an intuitive message that the woman's day was not going to get any better and would most likely lose her job after losing her temper during the meeting with her boss. Macy said nothing, knowing that it was not her place to provide that kind of information to anyone unless asked.

To minimize receiving negative messages about people in her proximity, Macy usually scanned the train car passengers before choosing a seat. She avoided those who had an agitated auric field and gravitated toward those who had smooth, calm energy. As autumn approached, it would become essential to carefully select whom she sat with as her ability to receive information increased exponentially in the fall.

Coughing. Sneezing. Fatigue. Worry. Sadness. Not one passenger with a positive outlook this morning. Maybe the weather had something to do with it; yet the rain was needed and people should be happy to have it. The sound of a cell phone playing "Beethoven's Fifth" rang out over the low rumble of the train and jarred Macy out of her thoughts.

"Hello?" someone shouted into the phone, "I'm on the train."

One of Macy's pet peeves was the use of cell phones in public places. The conversation was overheard by all, the talker making no attempt to lower her voice or end the call. Macy located the talker and focused on the cell phone. She forced energy toward the phone with the thought that the reception would go out and the call would end.

"Hello? Hello?" shouted the caller, then the closing of the cell phone and a heavy sigh. Macy discovered her ability to disable cell phones by thinking about disrupting the signal a few months ago. She was practicing to be able to block signals to the train car altogether.

Quiet. The hour ride took her from the suburbs of Bucks County, through the depressed areas of North Philadelphia, before arriving in Center City. Her years of riding the same train made her familiar with the other regular passengers. She knew at which stops they got on and off. She rarely saw anyone from her office on the train. It was better that way. She could prepare for work or decompress after a long day without having to speak to anyone.

The conductor called for Suburban Station. Macy rose from her seat and followed the other commuters out of the train and to her building. At the office, Macy sat at her desk, clenching her jaw, and wondering how she allowed herself to be working in such a poisonous environment. She could feel the negative energy of her co-workers; the fear that they lived with each day as they worried about the stability of their jobs. Mustering a shield of white light from head to toe, Macy attempted to dispel the dark emanations of those who postured themselves for selfish gain in this cutthroat business. It was becoming difficult to tolerate the pettiness and incompetence that surrounded her on a daily basis. Unfortunately, her job required her to interact on a continuous basis with everyone in the operations group. From the clerks to the presidents, there were very few benevolent spirits. Her power here was time-limited and conditional, dependent upon the whims and actions of those above her.

Walking down the center aisle, amidst the rows of cubicles, she could feel the different energies radiating from those who occupied them. The thickness and pervasiveness of the energy in each cube varied: some felt static and disordered, the energy spiking unpredictably. Others felt robotic and neutral, while others felt empty, totally lacking in motivation, thought, or drive. Most had sequestered themselves, not open to interacting with others, not wanting to disclose themselves to anyone around them. Macy recognized this as a symptom of fear and a lack of confidence. These people had little encouragement in their lives, and the work environment they faced each day was exacerbating their weakness.

Most of the senior management brought with them all of the insecurities it had taken a lifetime to develop and so preyed on those who felt even more helpless than they themselves did. Macy shuddered.

Even though she had risen above the rank and file, it required her to spend more time in this place with these people than she would have liked. Her success in business did not feel like a reward. If it had not been for her ability to collect information using other than the normal five senses, she might feel that her work was worthwhile. Going deeper than a superficial understanding of the world made her dissatisfied with what she had achieved. Her work was not meaningful in the scheme of what the world needed. Macy knew that with the powers she possessed, it would be possible to dedicate herself to a much nobler cause. But the money lured her away from her spirit and imprisoned her within the confines of her expenses. She had grown accustomed to a level of living afforded by her six-figure salary and liked it.

Macy had hand-selected her team of direct reports using what she knew of their skill sets, coupled with the nature of the energy that surrounded them. There was an elevated level of dedication among her team members. They thrived under her direction. Fostering open communication, their brainstorming sessions were productive and ripe with innovative ideas that were readily implemented. The offices of her team members where made warm and bright by the light they exuded. It was apparent that these people were open and flourishing within themselves.

In the twelve years that she had been with Sandlock Corporation, Macy had risen to the position of vice president of northern operations. Capable, intelligent, and highly intuitive, she was the only female to have moved up to a position of such authority. The male-dominated company valued Macy's ability to determine and accomplish a specified goal, usually under budget. She let nothing get in the way of completing her assignments. If there was an initiative that needed to be launched, Macy was where the division presidents placed their confidence. At times, Macy would be instructed to head in one direction, yet her highly developed intuition would tell her to move in another. She repeatedly identified strategic moves with a high degree of accuracy, even when it required going against one of the division presidents. In the beginning, they took offense to her objections; however, the accuracy of her predictions was undeniable, and they finally accepted the fact that she "just knows" what is going to happen.

Macy had discovered her abilities as a psychometrist when she was ten. She touched her father's pipe and received a mental impression of a woman who was her mother's age, but not her mother. The image had quickly faded. It took practice to be able to hold the images that came to her by holding different objects. Macy practiced in secret;

people would be frightened if they realized all of the things she had learned about them. People tried to project a different image of themselves rather than being more truly who they were.

Macy used her ability to learn about the people she worked with: their intentions, motivations, and fears. She took the information and used it to accomplish her goals. In general, she knew more about these people than she cared to. Shallow and lacking in integrity, to read their pens and palm pilots gave her a headache. Most nights she went home and performed a complete cleansing ritual to remove the residue. She tried to limit her exposure to their vibrations as an act of self-preservation. A steady diet of intense negativity would have detrimental physical side effects. To stay healthy, she protected herself when playing in their sandbox.

Today she was distracted from the normal issues of work. The supernatural events of late weighed heavily and she found it difficult to concentrate. The low-grade anxiety was familiar. It meant that a shift was about to occur and things would never be the same.

⚋ 8 ⚋

Macy was lost in the novel she was reading, when the conductor jerked her out of her trance. "Next stop, Jenkintown!" he yelled.

Macy did not notice the passengers boarding the train until she heard a jovial "Morning, Macy!" She looked up to see the smiling face of Ethan Talbot, a new director in her division. "Morning, Ethan," she returned. To her relief, he kept walking down the aisle to find a seat in the back of the train. Odd. Maybe he missed his usual train or just decided to board onto a different train car today, which would explain why in the weeks he had been employed at Sandlock Corporation she had never seen him on the train until now. Hopefully it would not be a regular encounter.

Ethan seemed likable on the surface, but Macy picked up an underlying energy in Ethan that she did not care for. He would say anything to be agreeable or to get people to like him, and then he would do whatever suited him. In his position as director of marketing, he quickly adopted a survival plan for this corporate environment: Tell people what they wanted to hear. Don't take responsibility for anything. Self-absorbed and a favorite among the single women in the office, Ethan used his charm and good looks to take full advantage of every situation. Macy was one of the few that were on to him. Bottom line—she did not trust him.

The potent protective shield Macy deployed, when she realized it was he, impressed Ethan. He watched as a cocoon of white light surrounded her and a solid sheet of energy that looked similar to steel shot up between them. Ethan was unable to probe her with his energetic tentacles. He was hoping to pierce the armor Macy kept so skillfully intact throughout the day by taking her by surprise, but was caught off guard himself by her quick response. Victoria had warned him that it would not be easy to keep watch on Macy. His mission would require the use of all of his occult abilities, including his natural gift of mind-reading.

One of the reasons Victoria had recruited Ethan Talbot into her coven was his talent for manipulating others. Strategically placed at

Sandlock Corporation, Ethan was able to observe Macy Vincent. He was skilled enough to pick information from Macy's mind when she was unaware of his presence. Victoria had seen potential in Ethan and took him under her wing, bringing his magical education to a whole new level. She knew rites and techniques that were not in any of the occult books Ethan had come across.

Victoria's effortless ability to astrally project was one of the prized teachings she afforded him. He had been tempted to check out Victoria as an astral voyeur. She was naturally provocative, and Ethan was incessantly drawn to her oozing sexuality. Ethan found Victoria's pale skin and long dark hair to be quite stunning. He also found himself to be an exceptionally attractive specimen, making the two of them, in his mind, physically compatible. Although his desire was strong, his fear of being discovered was stronger. He made the mistake of revealing his attraction to Victoria, and his sexual advances were met with disdain. A demonstration was necessary to teach him boundaries, so she cast a spell to temporarily paralyze his arms. He understood the lesson of the futility of future attempts at unauthorized groping. There was no telling what she would do to him as punishment for a second attempt.

In ancient times, the Triad Witches were considered great beauties; yet no man dared to touch them. Admired from afar, they were revered and respected. Their great power was feared and accepted. No one, not even the dullest among the citizens, would consider taking a chance to satisfy the carnal desires the Triad Witches sparked. It made no difference to Victoria if Ethan continued to covet her, as long as he remembered that she was as lethal as she was eye-catching. Ethan's persistence forced her to create a menacing energetic presence. If he chose to continue questioning her authority and attempting to couple with her, he would be committing spiritual suicide. She simply absorbed the life force of those who did not comply with her wishes until they collapsed. There would be no remorse.

There were safer targets. He would not mind astrally visiting a few attractive women at the office instead. They would be unaware of his presence, unless he chose to reveal himself.

Macy's vice presidential status limited his opportunities to be around her during the day. Their responsibilities did not intersect, and so it was difficult to have cause to be in Macy's proximity. Harder still was not knowing what he was watching and listening for. Victoria has simply instructed him to report any behavior or statements that were out of the ordinary. Ethan did not know Macy well enough to distinguish odd from normal behavior, but Victoria was High Priestess of the coven and he would do what she said.

He walked to the back of the train car and took a seat next to a sleeping Temple University student who had positioned her book bag considerately on her lap leaving the seat next to her vacant. Ethan knew that she would be getting off the train in a couple of stops, and then he would have the seat to himself. Settled in, Ethan's thoughts turned once again to Victoria. She had many secrets that Ethan hoped to have revealed to him. He did all he could to earn Victoria's trust and stroke her ego. One day he would be as powerful as she and start his own coven. He should have been high priest by now, but she made him wait.

Certain abilities were out of his grasp. One action in particular was most startling, that being the job at Sandlock Corporation. He had tried repeatedly to obtain employment there with no success. Once Victoria applied her magic, Ethan had a job with them by the following week, with no further application necessary. Ethan suspected that Victoria's capabilities ran far beyond what she was willing to show him. Her lessons stressed timing and the use of available energies in working a spell—"riding the tide", as she put it. He needed to be patient and allow things to unfold in their own time.

"Suburban Station," yelled the conductor. Ethan stood up and visually searched for Macy, but she was already gone. The crowd of people exiting the train engulfed her, protecting her from his probing view.

Macy quickly scurried up the steps into Suburban Station. She walked fast and forcefully to keep ahead of Ethan. She had no desire to start her day feeling his slimy energy field on her.

Ethan allowed himself to go with the flow of exiting passengers. With the moon in Taurus, it was time to seek pleasure, not rush, and Ethan was all about self-gratification. Ethan's energetic stride was typical for a Friday morning in anticipation of the weekend's rituals. They had the effect of recharging him with a fresh sense of purpose.

He had been working at Sandlock Corporation for a few weeks now. Most of the faces were familiar at this point, and he had hit the ground running, achieving beyond the expectations of his boss, Bill Jenkins. Bill was fond of wordlessly patting him on the shoulder and nodding his head in approval as he walked by. Jenkins was pleased at his hiring decision and was saved the embarrassment of selecting the wrong candidate. He liked the way Ethan made it a point to meet everyone and get to know his co-workers.

Ethan's co-workers easily succumbed to his manipulations and became unknowing participants in his plan. Ethan discovered that most people do not take personal initiative and, thereby, opened themselves to the forces he thrust upon them. They had become pawns he could shift at will, and the possibilities were endless. It never ceased to amaze him that those without purpose far outnumbered those who took charge of their own destinies. The puppets were plentiful, and the damage he could inflict was limited only by his imagination.

Ethan's interactions did not make for many friendships and created quite a few adversaries. He was sensitive enough to discern that caution was required in his dealings with Macy. She could easily brandish an attack designed to diminish his power. After his encounter on the train, he knew that she was well aware of the nature of energy and its effects. He told Victoria that he could feel her moving through the building. Ethan was disturbed to encounter a spirit who was, at the very least, his equal in the workplace. He didn't want to get involved with the energy coming from Macy. She was a formidable being. To provoke her could mean that power being directed at him. Ethan had been careful not to reveal himself to Macy, yet she had picked up on his muddy aura despite his best efforts.

Getting in the middle of two powerful women was not the smartest move in the world. He was wary of Macy's strength and fearful of Victoria's wrath. Ethan had grown to understand and accept Victoria's power, but was still uncomfortable with the idea of a woman being more powerful than him. Never had he run across such strength, coupled with the power to use it. Victoria instructed him to keep a piece of lapis lazuli with him for protection. The lapis would help to strengthen his spiritual energy and fend off the attempts at destroying his ability to complete his mission. Taking direction not being Ethan's strong suit, the gemstone was left uncharged, buried in his desk drawer.

He thought about retrieving it before fulfilling his task.

His mission, as dictated by Victoria, was to deliver a carefully selected gift to Macy. The item came from Harry's Office Supplies where Sandlock Corporation ordered its stationery needs, a new nameplate for Macy's desk that looked exactly like the old one, but with a twist; Victoria had infused it with her special brand of disruptive influence. Ethan relished the task, for he resented Macy's success and wished to please Victoria. He was determined to deliver this special contribution to Macy's demise without consideration of the consequences.

Attempts to dethrone her had met with adversity, for Macy's ability to protect herself energetically was the strongest he'd ever encountered. Her auric field could fill any room she stood in, and Ethan had been unable to break through to wreak havoc as he had done to so many others. His abilities were impressive, having successfully discredited three co-workers who were his direct competition for promotion. Macy was altogether different. Her motivations were for the good of the business rather than for herself. She actually cared about those she directed and her positive attitude completed the protection from Ethan's cosmic assaults.

With the others, it was simple to break through their thin veil of secret desires, to implant fear and doubt in their own abilities, and finally to crush their fantasies of success. The current goal of presenting this insidious gift to Macy would be a challenge; she was not one to readily trust someone, especially Ethan. He had been caught several times with inconsistencies. Macy was good at uncovering the truth. She was an astute observer and had many eyes and ears working for her.

While she was in a lunch meeting, Ethan slipped into her office unseen by Macy's team and exchanged the mundane nameplate with the charged one. He left feeling quite proud of himself and looking forward to watching the results of his deed.

Macy returned from the meeting, frustrated at the shortsightedness of her peers. She was thankful to have only a few more hours before starting the weekend. Macy checked e-mails that had come in during the meeting. She had the sense that something was not right in her office. She looked around and saw that everything was as she left it. Pen, letter opener, unopened mail, yet something felt different. The cloak of peaceful energy she tried to maintain within her office space had changed. It felt heavy and disturbing. Ethan watched from the hallway as Macy rubbed her forehead and temples, looking a bit piqued. She tried to ignore the sensation, but found herself snapping at one of her direct reports and being impatient on the phone. A general agitation filled her office, and she knew that a deliberate shift had been orchestrated.

Macy closed her office door and started to energetically scan all of the objects in the room—the bookcase, the snow globe on her desk, her nameplate. Her nameplate! The energy around it looked dark and she knew that this was the culprit. She reluctantly picked it up and closed her eyes. Sharp pain and bright light filled her head. She dropped the nameplate and put her hands to her forehead. Macy pulled her protective shield around her and filled it with green light to heal the damage. She asked her spirit guides to remove the harmful energy in the nameplate and to allow her to see the person who charged the object.

Her spirit guides gave her a message that it was done. Macy picked up the nameplate once again and opened to the information contained within it. A vision of a beautiful, dark-haired woman, tall and slender with pale skin came into her mind's eye. The woman's dark eyes looked so familiar. "Victoria Perry," her mind received the response.

Macy knew she had to discover why Victoria would seek to harm her. She wondered who put the nameplate in her office. It had to be someone in the office for it to have appeared after lunch and not before. Her senses were tingling. She vowed to keep her psychic ear to the ground to discover her saboteur.

* * *

Macy arrived at the Yardley station of the Southeastern Pennsylvania Transportation Authority's regional rail system at 4:25 pm. She had left work early, feeling weakened by the energetic hit she had taken from the nameplate. She had brought it home with her to see if she could derive any more information from it. It was in a canvas tote bag, which she left on her porch, not willing to contaminate her sacred space with its putrid energy.

It was always a relief to arrive here at the end of each weekday and be among the trees and the quiet of her quaint town. She pressed the electronic key to her silver Nissan 350Z and slid onto the gray leather driver's seat. The road on the ten-minute drive home was lined with mature maples, overhanging the street. They colored the evening twilight with bright orange and yellow. The tension began to seep out of her and her breathing deepened with each mile closer to home. Pulling into the brick driveway, she smiled at the stone English Tudor home.

Macy had always wanted a house like this, and had finally achieved the financial wherewithal to be able to comfortably afford it. The slate roof gave her the feeling of being in a rural English countryside, free from the static and tension of the city and its residents. A sense of overall well-being and warmth engulfed her. The winding path to her mahogany and leaded glass front door topped off her contentment as she slid the key into the bolt and granted herself access to her sanctuary.

Macy filled her home with elegant accoutrements, both new and antique. Each previously owned piece was carefully screened before being selected to become part of her refuge. It was challenging to go antique shopping, as Macy feared that touching items with a negative history could set off a flurry of unsettling images right there in the store. She let herself be drawn to certain pieces and considered them from afar before evaluating them with touch. Her selection process insured that nothing that made its way into her abode could conjure distressing images. That is what made this place so special to her: the total lack of negativity. The décor combined carved wood with stone to create a beautifully comfortable retreat. This environment helped her to tolerate the heavy energy at work, the place where she earned the money that enabled her to live this way.

She put her keys on the marble-topped table in the entry foyer and hung her Louis Feraud coat in the closet. Taking a deep breath, she pulled in the peacefulness of her surroundings, thanking God, as she did daily, for this perfect place. She envisioned a light supper and a good book yet could not get free of the psychic attack that occurred that afternoon. She decided to give Cassandra and Alexis a call.

*   *   *

Macy knew she needed more information about her enemy, Victoria Perry, and turned to the nameplate from her office. She went to her front porch to retrieve the object and walked with it down the side path to the backyard. She needed to perform this information retrieval outside so as not to release Victoria's negativity into the house.

Macy looked at the bag, reluctant to be hit with the harmful energy from the nameplate. Victoria's malice was clearly evident in the charging of the object. Sadness washed over her as she remembered that Victoria, as Amira, had once been her friend. Macy wondered what had changed to make her want to hurt the three other witches. She was compelled to energetically protect herself before touching the nameplate.

She planted her feet firmly on the ground and raised her arms to the sky. In her mind's eye she saw white light pouring down upon her, coating her aura. Macy beamed the light to extend to the trees on all sides of her. From the core of the Earth she pulled orange light into the bottoms of her feet and inside her body. She was now protected from above and grounded from below. Confident that she was ready to address the nameplate, she reached her hand into the bag and pulled it out and held it firmly in both hands.

Head bowed, she began. "I ask for information about Victoria Perry from the life we lived together. Whatever knowledge is deemed most critical, I accept," she whispered to the Universe.

Macy felt her body buzzing as she held the object. It showed her darkness and the spirits that dwelled within that darkness. She saw clouds and felt the cloaking spell Victoria had placed on the object. Macy knew that when an individual charges an object, a part of herself is imbedded, along with the original intention, so she persisted in clearing the distractions and opening to the information. Finally, she opened the way to the facts she sought.

It came through that Victoria's name was Amira. With her dark hair and dark eyes, she exemplified the shadow realm occupied by the dead. She was named to dominate and direct those around her to serve her purpose. She was the commander of the North, aligned with the element of Earth and the Wind of Mysteries. Her power came at midnight. Amira's parents had been chosen to produce a child whose energies would balance out the light of the other three. The couple's expertise focused on the realm of the dead. Each month Nanna Sin rested in the underworld where he decreed the fate of the dead, and Amira's parents were charged with understanding Sin's time there.

Qadir was chosen to teach Amira. He imparted knowledge of demons and dark forces. Amira opened to his teachings willingly and embraced the dark side.

The nameplate slid from her hands, and Macy returned to the present. Amira had succumbed to the dark energy available to her. Macy did not believe that there was no light to be found within her. Even on the darkest nights, a bit of starlight shines through. Macy wanted to release this light within Victoria Perry. The difficulty would be Victoria's reluctance to open. Macy could not force it and Universal law prevented her from interfering in another's path without permission. Macy considered the reason that this information was coming forth now. A situation was brewing, and she was in the middle of it.

"I thank the Universe for the information bestowed upon me and close the window on the opening created to obtain it."

Macy put the nameplate back into the bag and propped it up against the wall of the house. While the object felt somewhat diffused, she still did not want the resentful energy present in her abode. She went inside and took a shower to clear the energy of the psychic session. Salt scrub and lavender served to cleanse and calm the energy she had dealt with this morning. It would ready her for the next session with Alexis and Cassandra.

Refreshed, she went to the kitchen to brew some tea and have a light supper. Food was a good way to ground after being psychically open.

* * *

The doorbell rang and rang, one chime after the next. Macy opened the door to find an excited Alexis pushing the buzzer, anxious to share her discovery. She told Macy what Maxine had given her and handed her the paper. Macy's eyes widened as she read. Cassandra arrived soon after, and they told her about the new information. All three were bursting with excitement.

They gathered around the table in the conservatory. A white pillar candle was placed in the center and lit, along with a stick of sandalwood incense. The women placed their hands flat on the table and spread their fingers, all hands joined by pinkies and thumbs. Alexis led them through deep breathing exercises. Cassandra took over and asked for them to receive a vision. All were in complete synchronicity, breathing deeply in rhythm, eyes closed to the material world. Smoke from the incense swirled around the candle flame, making it flicker in the otherwise darkened room.

Fog rolled across their internal sight as the Witches simultaneously tuned into the vision; they were of one mind.

In the years of preparation to fulfill the role of guardians, they were schooled in all forms of The Craft. They were assigned educators in the occult arts in a special chamber prepared for their arrival. The brick walls were covered with shimmering fabric and the floor was painted with a compass denoting the four directions with Sin's symbol of the crescent moon in the center. Cribs were placed at each point of the compass and the babies placed at their proper directions. The high priests and priestesses gathered around the perimeter of the room to bear witness to the assigning ceremony. The children were very special, holding the balance of the world in their hands, and so their teachers were carefully chosen. Instruction in the occult arts was essential in order to develop their special gifts. The teachers must be adept at reading the psychic attributes of each child to properly nurture their talents and prepare them to use their enormous powers to protect the Scrolls of the Four Winds.

The assigning ceremony began, and the teachers of the temple came forward. They were dressed in white and wore sashes of various colors corresponding to the vibrational alignments of each direction. The Temple Elders had spent much time considering the attributes of the instructors and how they meshed with the special qualities of the children. With many capable professors to choose from, the Elders considered the temperaments as well as the knowledge base of each one.

In turn, each tutor stepped forward, bowed to the Council of Elders, and took his or her place behind the appropriate cradle. The infants looked up at their teachers, smiling, already forming an energetic connection with them. The gaze that held between infant and teacher was the first lesson in creating a bond between humans using the eyes as the conduit. With first impressions completed, each teacher reached out and put his or her right hand upon the solar plexus of the student. Palms firmly planted on the children, the teachers released a bolt of energy, establishing a stronger link with the child. It was the energetic signature that would allow them to communicate over great distances.

With guidance from their teachers, their powers blossomed beyond the abilities of any who had come before them. Each proved to have special gifts that were specially developed once identified. Mind control, divination, evoking spirits, sensing energetic patterns, drawing power from the moon, Psychometry, and healing were among their many talents. Individually they were formidable beings, capable of all sorts of magical conjurations. Together their power multiplied exponentially. They could generate an energetic field that could hold back a storm—or create one. Fixed on a target, this shield was impervious to all forms of negative attacks, physical or psychical. At age twenty-one, they were ready to fend off every form of energetic attack upon the scrolls.

The message made all the sense in the world. They were today who they had always been, in their past life as in this one. In the present, they still embodied all that their ancient teachers instilled.

"Where are they now?" Alexis exclaimed. "If we're here, they must not be far."

"Not necessarily. Just because we stayed together, along with Victoria, doesn't mean our teachers made it this far with us," reasoned Macy.

"Well, maybe, maybe not," considered Cassandra. "Our teachers were instrumental to the development of our powers. It is possible that they would continue to keep an eye on us."

"We didn't even know who we were until recently. They may have lost their memories as well, memories of who they are and of us," said Macy.

"I hope not," said Alexis. "To reconnect with my teacher is my fondest dream."

≠ 9 ≠

Alexis walked down Main Street toward home. Her daze was broken by the smell of hazelnut coffee wafting from the café she had just passed. The place was small, with two bistro tables positioned in each corner. The six customers waiting for service at the counter filled the coffee shop to capacity. Alexis took her place in line and read the menu on the back wall. Hazelnut had drawn her in, but she wanted to make sure that was what she wanted.

"Your first inclination is usually the right one," said a voice from the corner table.

Alexis looked over and saw a pale woman with dark hair and piercing dark eyes, then gazed about to see whom the woman had been speaking to.

"I was talking to you, my dear."

Eyes wide, brows lifted in surprise, Alexis was too startled to say anything. "Get your coffee and come sit with me," coaxed the woman.

Alexis did as she was told. Sitting with her steaming cup of hazelnut decaf in front of her, she stared into the woman's eyes, waiting for an explanation.

"I've been waiting for you," she said.

"You have? I don't even know you."

"But I know you. I am the one you seek," insisted the woman.

"How can I be looking for someone I never met before?" questioned Alexis.

"We have all met before. Many incarnations make no one a stranger. That aside, you requested a teacher, did you not?"

Alexis was taken aback. "How did you...?"

"How did I know that? The teacher appears when the student is ready. Isn't that how the old saying goes?" The woman smiled.

"Well yes, but..."

"You need a teacher to expand your knowledge of The Craft, isn't that so, Alexis?"

Her jaw dropped. "You know my name..."

"I know your name and many other things, my dear. I offer private lessons for exceptional students. I feel that you have many gifts that have yet to be tapped into. You lack confidence. You require guidance."

Alexis felt as though this woman knew her from the inside. She had a strange fluttery feeling as the woman's voice washed over her in velvety waves. A sip of coffee helped to keep her grounded and pushed the floating feeling away. It returned as the woman continued to speak.

"I am Victoria, here to help you achieve your most cherished dreams."

"Victoria, as in *Victoria's Antiques?*"

"The same."

"You sold my friend an incense burner," Alexis said in a suspicious tone, and then catching herself commented, "It was really beautiful."

"All of the objects in my store are specially selected. There is something to appeal to each person who comes through my door." Victoria's dark eyes cast a heavy shadow over Alexis.

Careful, Alexis warned herself. "So how much would these lessons cost me and what would I learn?"

Victoria saw a cobalt-blue pentagram between Alexis' eyebrows. She was protecting her third eye from Victoria's probing. "A practical girl, I like that," grinned Victoria. *So, she had begun to remember.* "Whatever you can afford to pay. As far as the content of the lessons, we will build upon your basic knowledge, beginning with casting circles and closing gateways. When evoking spirits, great care is needed."

"You don't have to convince me!" Alexis said as she recalled her ghostly mishap. She accepted the fact that Victoria seemed to know all about her. "Where would the lessons take place?"

"My store. I have a room in the back that I use to teach."

"Then I'm not your only student?"

"There are others, each hand selected by me."

"Will we all be in the same class?"

"Each of you are in varying levels of development, so at this time, your lessons will be private."

"I hope to meet them one day."

"We shall see. Can you come tomorrow evening at 7 pm?"

"I'll be there."

* * *

Maxine was anxious to get off work. She worried about Alexis and needed to get to her before Amira did. The library closed at 9 pm, too late to be knocking on her door uninvited. Her shift ended at 5 pm tomorrow. She would head straight to Alexis' house after work. Maxine projected a forced smile as she took the pile of books from the next patron.

* * *

Alexis walked home with thoughts of Victoria filling her mind. She could not shake the funky feeling that started when she began talking to Victoria. Even though red flags were going off at every turn, she still agreed to meet tomorrow evening. An odd trance had overtaken her, mesmerized by Victoria's voice, her eyes penetrating every neuron of Alexis' brain, forcing her to say yes. The focus now was to get home and clear her head and her aura of the persistent shadow that Victoria cast down upon her in the coffee shop. It clung to her, making her feel sluggish and invaded.

It was twilight by the time she arrived home. Alexis trudged up her front steps and onto the porch. She felt relief as she turned the key in the lock. Stepping inside, the cool, neutral shadows enveloped her, welcomed her. The encounter with Victoria left her feeling off balance. Macy's experiences with Victoria had been intense, and she did not trust that her own interactions would be any better. Alexis was unsure of Victoria's motivation, but her curiosity required that she find out. It was time to consult her guides. Whenever she was uncertain of a situation and how to proceed, she asked for information and guidance from them.

The correct frame of mind was essential for contact. An altered state of consciousness was most readily achieved using fire and sage. These helped her to immerse herself in the ritual and to let go of common reality. The many rituals she had conducted had darkened the makeshift fire pit in the backyard. A hole lined with large stones and surrounded by more of the same cradled dry logs that were split and easy to manage. She stuffed newspaper underneath to assist the flame in igniting the timber. As the fire grew, Alexis ran into the house and grabbed a bag of loose, white sage.

The fire was glowing nicely. After casting the circle and calling the quarters, she sat on a low beach chair she kept near the fire pit just for this purpose. A squirrel scurried across the yard, stopping to sniff the air, then continued on its way making rustling noises as it entered the bushes. Alexis maintained her concentration as she tossed a handful of sage into the flames. She asked to be cleansed of the negative energy that had fallen upon her. Smoke rose in great plumes. The neighbors were used to her cloudy rituals, so no need to worry about anyone calling the fire department. Standing up, she basked in its cleansing fragrance, holding her arms up and turning to allow it access to her entire body. White sage had a high vibrational pattern, able to dispel negativity. Satisfied, she sat back down and watched the smoke billow. It pooled around her, drawn to the harmful vibration that had attached itself to her. Alexis could feel it breaking down the darkness that surrounded her.

"I ask for a message about my current circumstances," Alexis spoke softly. She kept her intention general and open so as not to limit the type of message that came through. She did not have to wait long for an answer.

Use great caution at this time. Not all are friends. Your teacher will come to help you. Be open to her when she arrives. The voice came through as gender-neutral as always. It spoke inside her mind, objectively offering its wisdom. Alexis had learned to trust the voice; yet, this time she was confused. The advice seemed to be to open herself to Victoria as her teacher. She had such a bad feeling about it. She questioned her own judgment and wondered if her reaction to Victoria had been too harsh.

"What of Victoria? Can you give me information about her?" she sought to clarify.

You were together in ancient times. She was a friend and ally. The relationship changed. Forgiveness is the key to power.

Hard to give or get forgiveness in an unknown situation. "What is it that needs to be forgiven?"

She waited. The smoke dissipated. She called to the voice again. No message came. It was done. It was strange how the messages seemed to contradict her gut feeling. Alexis would meet with Victoria and hope that the answers presented themselves. She poured sand on the fire, and removed the circle, closing the portal behind her. The smell of sage smoke and burning wood permeated her hair and clothing. A shower would complete the cleansing.

She pulled off her top as she climbed the stairs to the second floor. She gave a head start to the hot water by turning on the faucets before removing the rest of her clothing. An old house had special quirks, like water taking a while to heat up. She piled her clothes on the bathroom floor and stepped into the steaming shower. It felt good to wash off the day.

Bathing was essential to remove the accumulated energies. Alexis was aware of it every time she was around people. It was difficult to avoid contact with the energy fields of others, and when they made contact, it felt heavy and alien to her own aura. She took her time, letting the hot water soak into her hair and gently massage her shoulders and upper back. She turned off the faucets and squeezed excess water from her hair. The thick, soft towels felt good on her skin. She finished by buffing moisture from her wet hair and wrapping the towel around her ample bosom, tucking it securely by the corner.

As Alexis entered her bedroom, she glanced at the unmade bed with its thick comforter bunched up in the middle, just as she had left it that morning. It looked remarkably like a person lying in bed on his left side, the right shoulder bunching the covers up into a small hill near the pillows. As Alexis considered this, she saw the covers move as though someone was pushing them off to start the day. The action revealed a handsome, dark-haired man, in his thirties, staring at her with wide eyes and a grotesque smile.

She had never seen this spirit before. Many apparitions came through her house, but this one was unfamiliar. He had a strange density to him, as though he were not from the other side of the veil. She tried to get a message from him, but was unable to pull anything but a sense of sarcasm and superiority. Her hands tested the front of the towel making sure it was closed, suddenly feeling as though the phantom was hoping to see her flesh.

She blinked as he sat up, not wanting to turn her back on him. The next cautious glimpse at the bed left it empty and innocuous. The abrupt departure was a relief, yet left her on-guard for the remainder of the evening. Never before had an apparition challenged her in such a bold manner. She vowed to cleanse the whole house with sage in the morning. She did not possess sufficient energy to dispel negativity after all that had transpired, and needed to rest before that sort of undertaking.

Alexis straightened the sheets and comforter so that they laid flat on the mattress and went to put the towels in the bathroom. She entered the bedroom once again and to her relief saw the bed unoccupied, unable to shake the feeling that what she saw was not a ghost. What else could appear to her in such a way? It could not be one of her guides, for their energy was benevolent. This specter seemed to be a conscious being, more solid than most. He seemed to be making fun of her. Alexis desperately needed to sleep before contemplating this further, but needed to calm the energy in the room first. She recited Psalm 23, clicked the television on for company, and quickly fell asleep.

≉ 10 ≉

Floating and weaving, bobbing and surfing, the autumn leaves came down from their perch. This autumn would go down in Heather's personal history as her greatest. Never again would she feel so close to others and so appreciated. Ethan and Victoria were dedicated and patient teachers, making sure her lessons were well learned. Halloween was less than a month away, and they promised it would be something really special, for it was a Witch's most powerful night when the veil between the worlds is the thinnest. Heather could not understand why Sandy and Helen did not accept Victoria's offer to join the coven. They were really missing out.

In the month that had passed since her first dinner with them, they taught her restraint, as well as the skill of draining someone to the last drop. She felt more powerful and in control than ever before, testing her abilities and practicing her lessons with abandon. Like proud parents, they reveled in her achievements. Ethan's special attention made her feel attractive and desirable. She began to hope that she would make the transition from pupil to lover in the very near future.

The lessons teaching her to read the thoughts of her victims were her favorite. Heather preferred it when Ethan took her out for her lessons, just the two of them. Sometimes she felt intimidated by Victoria. Through Victoria's smile and praise, Heather sensed a selfish purpose to her generosity. Besides, when she was alone with Ethan, he made her feel like she was the most important person in the world. To practice, they went to The Landing Restaurant on Main Street. There they could sit outside on the terrace overlooking the Delaware River. In this serene environment, she could open to the thoughts of those that dined around them.

"Relax. Take a deep breath and feel your Third Eye open. Choose a target and focus on getting information." Ethan would rub her shoulders as he instructed her, to assist her in moving to a trance state. Sometimes it would help her to relax. Other times it made her mind wander to having his hands on the rest of her.

Ethan was fully aware of the effect he had on Heather. He enjoyed manipulating her and feeding her fantasies about him. The decision had not yet been made as to whether he would sleep with her or not. She was attractive, yet needy, and he had no desire to fuel a dependent relationship. In the meantime, teasing her was fun, and it instilled loyalty to him. Whether or not Heather was loyal to Victoria was not his concern. Ethan saw the potential to use Heather for his own purposes. He would have Heather worship him, and he would start his own coven where he would be the High Priest.

"I'm focusing on the woman in the corner with the white top and striped pants. She's smiling and talkative. The man she is sitting with is a first date from one of those Internet dating services. She is thinking that his online profile information and photo do not match what she was seeing in person. 'How can I make a graceful exit,' is what she is thinking." Heather smiled. The information felt accurate. When she picked up on someone's thought thread, she spoke rapidly without hesitation.

"Excellent! I picked up the same thing! You're really catching on quickly," Ethan stroked her ego. He bestowed upon her the admiration and encouragement she had always longed for and, at the same time, was being completely truthful in assessing her progress.

Heather smiled more broadly. She loved hearing his praise. There was nothing she was unwilling to do for him.

"Now, pick a different target. I want you to practice scanning for disease and weakness," Ethan instructed.

Heather looked around. It was amusing that they were so unaware of what she was doing. Across the flagstone terrace, Heather spotted two women chatting intently. Their energy drew her curiosity, and she relaxed her eyes to be able to see their auric fields. Ethan and Victoria warned her about drinking energy from someone who had a low vibration, hence Heather would be weakened by taking the illness or angst into herself. Lord knew she had more than enough weaknesses already, so she heeded the advice with gusto. When scanning a room for victims, she chose those with strong energy fields that had no holes or dark spots.

There were times when Heather was tempted to drink from the powerful auras of Victoria and Ethan. Expert at shielding themselves from her psychic fangs, the task would be impossible. Even if she could break through the protective screen, she did not want to anger them by risking a drink without permission. She thought of asking for their consent, as energy from willing hosts felt much more potent than what she stole from unsuspecting donors. Yet she never broached the subject, not wanting them to feel that she was ungrateful and potentially be expelled from the coven. To be alone in the world once again would be the worst punishment imaginable. The coven provided purpose and camaraderie, learning and development.

Ethan sat looking at Heather, amazed at her fast progress. He mentally patted himself on the back, taking credit for the advancement of her psychic talents. He knew she did it for him, to impress him. He could feel her desire pulling at him. Ethan had been tempted more than once to take advantage of her longing. She did not look half bad now that he and Victoria had given her a makeover, both physically and spiritually. He wanted to teach her other ways to please him, but proceeded with caution. This was Victoria's little project, and he did not want to aggravate Victoria. She had given him the supernatural squeeze more than once, and it was not pleasant. It was apparent that he would not get anywhere sexually with "V" as he liked to call her within himself. She made it clear that she was off limits. Heather was another story. V would not mind if he released his tension on Heather; yet he was afraid that by doing so she would become a clinging vine. He would rather string her along to get her to do his bidding.

The assignment Victoria had given him of late was challenging and pleasant. He astrally projected himself into Alexis's bed just long enough to give her a start. It was difficult to maintain the apparition. To project his mind only was a much easier task, and he could sustain his view for as long as he liked. To make himself appear solid was another matter entirely. He had waited and watched in her bedroom before making himself solid. For that brief moment, he was delighted to catch her wearing only a towel. She was quite attractive, her long chestnut hair wet and clinging to her shoulders. The startled look on her face as he lay in her bed smiling at her was priceless. He wondered what V had in store for this delectable beauty.

* * *

Cassandra opened her doors at ten each morning, appointment book filled or not. Many times, customers walked in off the street, seeking her insights. This morning she took extra time clearing her studio and centering herself before seeing clients. She had received intuitive warnings for the last few days that something major was about to happen. The anxiety built as she waited. Information did not come at her command. She learned that it revealed itself when it was time. It was stronger today than the last couple of days, so her expectations of a revelation were high. The pressure of the pending magic pressed on Cassandra. To tolerate it, she surrounded herself with white light and grounded herself to the Earth with orange and yellow light.

Tea was another way to help her endure the wait, so she brewed a pot of lavender tea and sat peacefully sipping it while listening to the calming piano music of David Lanz. Steam rising from her teacup made a sudden deliberate swirl in the air just as two women entered the studio.

Cassandra greeted them warmly and asked how she could be of service.

"We are Sandy Halpern and Helen Cassavettes. Do you have some time to read us?"

"Certainly. How long would you like the readings to be?"

"Thirty minutes should be sufficient. Both of us at once."

Cassandra invited them into her reading room and went to get more cups for tea. Once everyone was comfortable, she began.

Cassandra pulled out two decks of cards and handed a deck to each woman. "Shuffle the cards and choose five."

They did as instructed and handed the five cards to Cassandra. She spread them with one card in the center and one card touching each corner. This she did for each set of five, creating two separate stars on the table. With a deep breath, Cassandra opened to the messages awaiting the women. As she let out the breath in a slow, steady stream, white light flashed in her mind, momentarily blinding her. As the light diminished, a scene came clear, as though she was witnessing it in real time, and was guided to speak:

We played in the temple gardens under the watchful eyes of our teachers. Even at times when we were unencumbered by lessons, our instructors observed our actions and guided us to remain consistent with Magical Laws in our thoughts and behaviors. They taught us to never forget who we were and to consider the Laws in all circumstances.

In the Law of Association, everything is connected and reacts to that which is imposed upon it. The Law of Balance, in which the mage practices energy conservation by exercising moderation in thought and action. The Law of Contagion, in that what has been in contact with each other continues to have an effect, even at a distance. The Law of Identification, where one entity assumes the characteristics of another. The Laws of Infinity, wherein there are infinite data and sources of information available to us, creating a circumstance that allows for an infinite number of perspectives or universes. The Law of Knowledge, in that understanding and wisdom allow for power and control. The Law of Self-knowledge, where to know oneself is the key to mastery and

Adepthood. The Law of Polarity assumes that all components can be separated into their opposites; everything contains dark and light, good and evil.

Our teachers gave us affection and encouragement. Amira's teacher, Qadir, did not provide his lessons in this manner, but rather encased her in darkness and discipline. She tried to fit in with the rest of us, but had difficulty shedding the influence of her teacher. The Laws of Identification and Association were exemplified in their relationship.

Cassandra's eyes were glazed as she looked at the women. "Huda, I have missed you!" She embraced her teacher.

"It is good to see you as well, Iman. You remember your lessons well."

"And Akilah! Macy, uh I mean Uzma, will be thrilled to see you!"

Sandy smiled. "It has been too long."

Fully awakened, Cassandra felt as though she could see clearly for the first time in this life. "I fear I have been in a deep slumber. My life until now feels as a dream, yet many of your lessons stayed with me."

"You have been under a powerful enchantment that is only now unraveling. For centuries, you and the rest were subdued by Victoria's desire to have you forget your true purpose," explained Helen.

"Now that you have awakened, there is great danger to you and the others. Where are Macy and Alexis?" asked Sandy.

"Macy is at work. I'm not sure where Alexis is. Maybe she's at home. We can call them," offered Cassandra.

"Sandy and I have to go to work. Try to get everyone to meet here at 6 pm."

* * *

Alexis wanted to be prepared for her meeting with Victoria, so she left the house early to gather some supplies. White sage and ritual candles were staples, and she was out of both. Her guidance told her that performing a cleansing and protection ritual before encountering Victoria was a good idea. She could not help feeling conflicted about going over there. She hoped that by doing so she would find some answers. This enigma drew her in, and Alexis wanted to know how she fit in. The desire for knowledge around the Mysteries drove her as well, for she had felt Victoria's power and control. She, too, wanted the ability to wield her energy by force of will.

In all of the self-study she had done and in lessons with her grandmother, the development of will and knowledge of oneself were paramount to the ability to perform magic and to connect with the Universal Energy. Text after occult text pointed in the same direction.

By simply reading a spell, the mage could not expect to get desired results. The power was within the practitioner. The ability to focus and concentrate plus the use of imagination and the mental capacity to clearly envision the goal were interconnected. This approach felt right to her. She had learned to trust what felt right. When something was not correct or counter to her path, she felt anxious, and her physical body reacted disapprovingly to the decision or thought.

There was a blended sense about Victoria. On the one hand, Alexis felt vulnerable to be exposed to such magical muscle. On the other hand, she sensed something deeper inside of Victoria that seemed to reach out in camaraderie. It was as though Victoria was enticing her into friendship by offering the knowledge she desired. There was a part of Alexis that felt sad for Victoria. The loneliness and melancholy emanated from her in tiny waves, detectable only to someone with the gift to sense and interpret energy. Maybe there was a chance they could give something valuable to each other: knowledge for Alexis; friendship for Victoria.

She walked down the concrete steps and pushed open the door to *Gypsy Heaven*. The girl behind the counter was dressed in black and wore silver jewelry imbedded with large chunks of onyx. Her hair was black with streaks of unnatural red. Alexis knew that to dress in anything other than black would put this worker at risk, being exposed to the energies of so many practicing witches throughout the day. For those who practice The Craft or other forms of energy work, their auric fields reached far beyond the average six inches of non-practitioners.

"Merry meet. My name is Sandy. Can I help you find anything?" She recognized Mina's long chestnut hair and intense dark eyes. She had not changed that much over the centuries.

"I know where everything is, thanks," replied Alexis. She walked over to the basket of white sage bundles and selected three. The display of ritual candles had every color of the rainbow and then some. She chose five each of black, white, and purple.

"Will there be anything else today?" said Sandy, as she calculated the total. "We have some incredible new stones. You may want to check out the lapis lazuli."

Alexis looked down into the glass case that housed the stones. The image of a silver box loaded with lapis lazuli flashed across her mind. Sandy saw the startled look on her face.

"Something... it looks so familiar, yet I never..." said Alexis, still grappling with the vision.

Sandy mulled over her authority to release Mina from her etheric bonds. She had felt Hala in the area and wondered if she should wait for her or if circumstances warranted her immediate awakening. She considered Alexis, standing there awash in confusion. In ancient times, Mina was an eternal seeker of knowledge. Sandy knew Mina would have a strong desire to awaken, despite the absence of her teacher, Hala.

Sandy lit a charcoal disk and plopped a small chunk of copal resin onto it. The thin smoke moved with the light air current in the room. The scent reached Alexis, and her eyes glazed over. Sandy took the largest piece of lapis lazuli from the case, put it in Alexis's hand, and closed her fingers around it. Alexis closed her eyes. She was in the temple; silken drapes fluttering against the stone walls, watching Macy carry the censer to the altar. *Not Macy*, she thought, *Uzma. My sisters, the Triad Witches, surround me. Iman, Uzma, Amira.* The incense smoke grew dense, filling the room with its aroma and ancient memories. *We are here to protect the scrolls, the four of us, together.*

"That's right," said Sandy. "You were meant to work together always."

Alexis opened her eyes and saw Sandy standing next to her as Akilah. "Akilah, thank you for helping me to remember."

Akilah smiled. "It's good to have you back. Iman has also been awakened. Only Uzma is left."

"And what of Amira?"

"Amira has been aware through the centuries. She is the reason the three of you lost yourselves across time. You have met her," Akilah's voice held a serious tone.

"Victoria. I am supposed to meet with her tonight. She offered to instruct me in the magical arts."

"The Dark Arts is more accurate. She has had her eye on you, creating mishaps in your spells. In this way, she has convinced you that it is dangerous to continue your practice of The Craft without a teacher."

Alexis had been wondering if she was incompetent in her abilities. This news, although disturbing, was a great relief. "We were meant to be together. What happened?"

"I believe it was Qadir's influence on Amira. He taught her jealousy, resentment, and selfishness, all attributes of the Dark Arts. As a result, she sought individual power by way of possessing the Scrolls of the Four Winds."

"She turned against us. That is what must be forgiven."

"Amira wanted total control, and still does. She did not wish to share the power among the four of you," Sandy explained.

"Maxine Ashcraft at the library was telling me about the scrolls. She said they were meant to stay together. Couldn't that be true of the four of us? We were meant to be together through time, united for a purpose."

"Maxine? She told you about the scrolls?"

"Yes, and about the Great Library of Alexandria, The Seven Evil Spirits, and The Seven Fires."

"Hala!" exclaimed Sandy. "She was your teacher in Ur. We must gather everyone tonight. Helen and I are scheduled to meet Iman at her studio at 6 pm, although I'm thinking that 5:30 pm is better. Cassandra is calling Macy at work."

"Should I still plan to meet with Victoria at 7 pm?"

"Yes. There is something you need to do that can only be accomplished in her presence. We will prepare you before you go. Can you contact Hala?"

"Absolutely."

* * *

Maxine was thrilled to see Alexis walk through the library entrance.

"Hello, Hala!" Alexis greeted her with a warm embrace.

"You know!"

"I just left Akilah. She calls herself Sandy in this life and works at Gypsy Heaven."

"Akilah! I thought I felt her nearby."

"We're meeting tonight at 5:30 pm at Cassandra's, uh, I mean Iman's studio. Can you be there?"

"Nothing could stop me!"

≠ 11 ≠

Everyone gathered at the appointed time. It was a family reunion. Energies were high and all were joyous to be together once again, despite the circumstances that brought them together. Cassandra had put together a light smorgasbord of Middle Eastern treats in celebration of their history together. Everyone delighted in the couscous, hummus, pita, and falafel. Plates in hand, they sat in a circle to get down to more serious matters.

"The situation at hand is critical. Samhain approaches and the veil will be the thinnest. It will be more difficult to stop Victoria at that time, given her mastery of the evocation of spirits," began Helen, Cassandra's teacher.

"We want to refresh your memories as to the circumstances that led up to Victoria's deception in ancient times, to prepare you for the confrontation that is on the horizon," continued Sandy.

Candlelight flickered against the walls as Maxine told the tale.

"The Scrolls of The Four Winds awaited their protectors at the Royal Library in the secret room built to preserve them. Physically protected by the Egyptian army and encased in solid silver vessels, the mystical scriptures had been energetically guarded by a group of specially ordained priests called the Order of the Mystics. Their power was limited to the immediate area in which they conjured a protective shield. The unexpected death of the most dominant Mystic weakened their protective shield and rendered it inadequate to protect the scrolls. The Triad Witches were immediately summoned to Alexandria. The remaining three Mystics continued to stand guard until you could arrive. As you traveled, the four of you assisted the Mystics in protecting the scrolls by beaming energy to the location where the scrolls were hidden.

"The energy that the three of you emitted was shining brightly. Suddenly there was a shift in vibration of the energy emanated by Amira. Uzma felt it first and knew that Mina and Iman could feel it, too; yet none of you spoke out against your childhood friend. Your gifts were highly developed and could identify negativity from a great distance. Mina was highly focused on learning the rituals associated with The Craft and felt prepared to do whatever was necessary to defend against dark spirits. Iman had ultimate faith in people and the belief that all are inherently good. The two of them had converted many an ill-willed soul to a positive purpose, so their confidence grew in the ability to help Amira through their magical skills. They innocently trusted those around them to do no harm, for they themselves would not seek to hurt anyone. Unwavering focus on the mission was the purpose they served in this moment. The ability to concentrate is what made you great sorceresses. The love and light you channeled is what made you exceptional individuals.

"Uzma vowed to protect the scrolls from the whispers of malevolence that came in waves from Amira. Pride would prevent Amira from ruining the mission of the Triad Witches. At the same time, Amira's self-importance threatened to harm the other members of the group. Movement on the deck above disrupted Uzma's thoughts. The Lighthouse of Alexandria, which sat on the island of Pharos, was visible from out at sea. Representatives of the Order of Mystics awaited your arrival at the Eastern Harbor, where the Great Library was located. You prepared to dock by pulling back on the protective energy field. The Mystics were to protect the scrolls on their own until you had been properly prepared to assume your vigil.

"The Mystics readied a welcome for The Triad Witches. Private bathing accommodations waited. The large pool was filled with clear water and spiked with lavender oil. Pots of myrrh resin burned in each corner of the room, purifying the energy of the space to protect and bless as you washed yourselves clean of the long journey. The cleansing was both physical and spiritual, releasing the tension, grime, and fear that had accumulated around you from the soldiers on the ship. Wrapped in soft, absorbent cloth, the four of you were led down a stonewalled tunnel. Torches lined the walls to light the way down the dark passage. You walked in silence. The arched wooden doors at the end of the passageway led to separate sleeping chambers.

"Each room contained a bed made of a woven mat covered in fine linen sheets. The mattress frame sat on legs in the shape of bird wings. At one end was a headrest wrapped in layers of cloth. A recessed space housed a limestone seat that sat above an earthenware bowl designed to hold human waste until servants emptied it. New gowns had been made of white, shimmering fabrics with sashes of red, yellow, black, and blue, representing the corresponding elements of the Four Winds— Fire, Air, Earth, and Water, respectively—and placed in each chamber. You chose your bedrooms in accordance with the elemental vibration of the chamber. Uzma vibrated to the element of Fire; Mina to Water; Iman to Air; Amira to Earth.

"Fatigued by the journey and by the amount of energy you had conjured along the way, you slept into the twilight of the following day. Properly rested, you sat at the dining table in the common area that joined the sleeping chambers and ate a simple meal of fruit and grain. Toward the end of the meal, the Mystic, Isam, joined you. He walked to the eastern wall and waved his hand over a crumbling spot in the mortar. A piece of the wall slid to the right and disappeared within the main wall, leaving an access door to another tunnel. You walked sixty feet down the corridor to a bronze door, heavily decorated with protective signs and symbols. There was no latch or doorknob. Isam waved his hands once again, and the door popped open.

"The room was fragrant with Frankincense and dimly lit. The three remaining Mystics sat in silence with heads bowed, focused on the silver box that sat on the pedestal between them. Imbedded with pieces of lapis lazuli and onyx, the box was surrounded by a faint glow. The box alone afforded some protection for the scrolls. Manufactured by craftsmen who specialized in magical amulets, boxes, and trinkets of all kinds, the box was designed to create a shield around the scrolls. The very nature of the materials it was made with enhanced its ability to be used as a sacred vessel for its supernatural cargo. Made of the potent protectors of pure silver, onyx, and lapis lazuli, the container could ward off evil and amplify the psychic power of the scrolls that lay within.

"Iman sensed the weakness of the protective field and the fatigue of the men who created it. Their balance had been thrown off by the death of the fourth Mystic assigned to the scrolls, leaving one direction unprotected. Sadness and defeat washed over Iman as she pulled these emotions from the men. By outward appearance, the casual onlooker would see no signs to indicate that the Mystics felt anything but peace and concentration."

"Iman's sense of others had grown stronger with practice. There were times when she intentionally closed herself from the sensation, as she could feel the emotional pain of others as though she were going through it herself. She was impressed that the Mystics had persisted in their duty to protect the scrolls despite their grief and their exhaustion," said Helen proudly, recalling the achievements of her student.

Maxine nodded and continued. "The Triad Witches took their places: Amira to the North, Uzma to the South, Iman to the East, and

Mina to the West. You raised your arms simultaneously, palms up to receive the power of The Source, fuel for the protective shield about to be conjured. Mist formed at the ceiling of the chamber, glowing with otherworldly light. It expanded to encompass the box and the Mystics. Floating down around the pedestal, the light grew brighter and seemed to become solid rather than vapor, coming to rest on the upturned palms of each Witch.

"Isam picked up a small beater and gently hit the ceremonial gong that stood just inside the doorway. The Mystics took in a long, deep breath and upon releasing it, removed their spell. With a reverent bow, the men moved slowly away from their positions, glad to be relieved of their duty. Without the fourth Mystic, it had been an arduous task to maintain the admittedly weak shield around the sacred scrolls. They were pleased to relinquish their watch to the powerful Triad Witches. The Mystics had never felt or seen such a forceful light as that generated by these four young women. Confident that the scrolls were left in good hands, they departed the chamber, looking forward to food and rest. The men out of the way, you extended your arms to shoulder height, then brought them gently down to your sides. Palms now facing the center of the circle, the light beamed directly at the target. Sitting on the seats positioned at each station, they began their long vigil."

Alexis chimed in, "I remember now, gazing at the chunks of lapis lazuli adorning the box. It was not surprising that the craftsmen who created the vessel chose lapis lazuli for its protective qualities. They were similar in size to the smooth oval lapis lazuli stone I had worn since birth, a gift bestowed by the high priestess of the Moon God Temple as a symbol of my given name, Mina. Too large for an infant, I grew into the stone's size; replacing the leather strap each time I outgrew the last."

Maxine was pleased that Alexis had begun to remember the past in such detail. Looking at Alexis, she spoke, "That's right, Alexis. Associated with the Element of Water, your affinity for lapis lazuli drew you to the West. Vibrating with the planet Venus, it brought love into your heart and spirit. The stone was believed to contain Divine power giving the wearer potent magical abilities including the power to heal, to protect, and to possess psychic awareness. Over time, you learned how to channel the power of the stone for the highest good of those around you, and using it to help protect the Scrolls of the Four Winds."

Maxine looked around the room at the others as she explained further.

"The lapis lazuli felt heavy on her chest, boring into her flesh as she pulled energy from it and directed it outward to mingle with the other three. Mina looked over at Amira to the North. Amira's concentration was unyielding and intense. The energy she produced was harsh compared to that being emitted by Iman and Uzma. The other two contributed smooth, benevolent light to the mix, aligning with Mina's own. Amira's forceful emanations seemed to flow separately from the others. The protective field was not compromised, yet the shield did not feel solid. There was darkness in the section of the shield created by Amira. Mina glanced over at Uzma in the South quadrant of the chamber. Her concentration was divided between generating the light and watching Amira.

"Uzma had long suspected that Amira was not of the same mindset as the other witches. Their lives had been joined since birth, yet Amira's path had taken a turn to the left. The days when the two ran hand-in-hand through the temple gardens were long gone. Amira avoided Uzma's touch, fearing Uzma's gift of Psychometry. A single touch allowed Uzma to intimately know the intent and motivation of a person. Those who were pure of heart had no hesitation in allowing her gentle touch to permeate their auric fields. Only people with hidden purpose were reluctant to permit such an invasion of privacy. Amira's disposition began to change as she spent more and more time with the priest, Qadir. Now that they were many miles apart, Uzma hoped that his influence would grow dim.

"In the East, Iman pulsed with a pale yellow light, pushing it up and willing it to spread across her quadrant. It glided smoothly to blend with the energy of the others. As the energy passed through her, Iman felt a giddy joy fill her. Moving energy allowed her to be closest to The Source; being intimate with the Divine filled her with happiness. The role the Triad Witches came to fulfill was an important one, and Iman was thrilled to be a part of it. The Scrolls of the Four Winds were too powerful to be left unguarded. In the wrong hands, they could create great upheaval in the world. No one person could possess them and not be corrupted by their power. Iman's attention turned back to the force that was flowing through her. Soon the flow would overtake all of you, rendering you unaware of your surroundings; its energizing qualities enabling you to continue the vigil for several days without rest or food. The Source nourished you and kept you awake for the duration.

"On the third day, rumbling on the ground above broke the trance. Dust and dirt shook down from the ceiling like powdered sugar through a sifter, sprinkling your hair and robes with fine, gray particles. The shield remained strong. Isam burst into the chamber, face red and wet with panic.

"'Emperor Theodisius ordained the destruction of all pagan temples and other structures in Alexandria. The Great Library is under attack!' Isam exclaimed. 'They are burning all of the scrolls contained in the library. We must not let them take the sacred box.'

"Isam was winded and sobbing. He bowed his head, and Amira seized the opportunity. Spreading her arms wide at shoulder length, she put forth a burst of dark energy and exclaimed, 'By the power of The Seven Evil Spirits, who come riding the storm of destruction, I call upon them to deliver the sacred scrolls unto me for my own purpose!'

"The three of you were taken off guard and lost your concentration, staring at Amira in horror. She continued chanting loudly, the darkness closing in, the chamber's floor violently shaking.

"'Raging storms, evil gods are they, ruthless demons, who in heaven's vault were created, are they, workers of evil are they, they lift up the head to evil, every day to evil, destruction to work.

Of these seven the first is the South wind.
The second is a dragon, whose mouth is opened wide
That none can measure.
The third is a grim leopard, which carries off the young.
The fourth is a terrible Shibbu.
The fifth is a furious Wolf, who knoweth not to flee,
The sixth is a rampant demon, which marches against god and king.
The seventh is a storm, an evil wind, which takes vengeance,
Seven are they; messengers to King Anu are they,
From city to city darkness work they,
Hurricanes, which mightily hunt in the heavens, are they
Thick clouds, that bring darkness in heaven, are they,
Gusts of wind rising, which cast gloom over the bright day, are they.'*

"A light wind began to blow in the underground chamber, picking up speed enough to blow your hair gently, then more violently so that it had to be pushed away from your eyes. Amira maintained her posture, reveling in the powerful gusts she had created. The flowing material of her grown pressed against her figure as she withstood the force of those she had evoked. Isam cowered in a corner, his arms protecting his head, powerless to intervene.

---

* Excerpt from *The Seven Evil Spirits*, R.C. Thompson, translator [The Devils and Evil Spirits of Babylonia, London 1903]

"The wind in the chamber had picked up speed and was whistling at a high pitch. Uzma looked at the others, and waved her arms to get their attention. Iman and Mina glanced over to her, reluctant to take their attention away from their wicked colleague. Bringing her hands to the prayer position in front of her heart chakra, Uzma nodded at the two of you, encouraging you to do the same. To stay grounded and focused was the only way to stand up against the mounting gloom conjured by Amira. The three of you in place, you bowed your heads and garnered a store of energy. Without an upward glance, you simultaneously spread your arms and released a sizable ball of white light that pushed the darkness away from the sacred vessel.

"Amira screamed, her rage momentarily diminishing her focus. Eyes sending hatred toward her three companions, she grounded herself as the wind swirled about the chamber without purpose, the demons awaiting direction from their mistress. She envisioned giant roots growing from the bottoms of her feet and digging down into the chamber floor, going into the core of the Earth itself. She could feel her fury subside and regained control. With chilling determination she chanted:

"'Your magical memory is wiped clean

For centuries you'll wander

Without knowledge you three will be lost

Your minds wander across a field, through a meadow, up a mountain

Knowing not where to stop, traveling far yet yielding not

To any clarity of thought, any one direction to flow

All of your energy has nowhere to go

Your dreams are scattered to the four winds

So many fragments reborn lifetime after life

Together yet apart, your journey is about to start!'

"Amira's hands gracefully orchestrated the demons she had conjured, moving them forcefully between her three sisters. Although you stood fast, desperately trying to maintain focus, the demons muddled your thoughts and fed on your energy until the ball of light diminished to a gray remnant of its former brilliance. Uzma watched helplessly as Iman and Mina fell to the floor. The world spun and the ground shook until she, too, collapsed under the power of the demon wind. Grains of dirt fell from the ceiling onto the jeweled vessel. Amira smiled in victory.

"'I dismiss all demons, energies, and spirits attracted by this ritual. Be prepared to return to serve my will when I command thee.' She clapped her hands twice and separated them, dispersing the current of evil.

"With the vessel under her arm, Amira threw open the chamber door. Isam made no move to stop her for fear of retaliation. Amira's eyes grew large as she stared at Isam, shooting daggers of doom toward his heart chakra. Isam stared in disbelief as he clutched his chest and went down on his knees, falling over into the rubble that coated the floor. Amira gathered the hem of her robe and lifted it to hasten her ascent up the steps, vigilant of encountering any of the Mystics on her way. She reached the top of the steps and smelled the destruction of the library, scrolls smoking and burning in every direction. Screams and shouting could be heard throughout the building. She had to find a safe place to hide until the attack subsided.

"Asking for guidance from her spirit protectors, she was shown a door that she had not noticed before. She pulled at the handle and saw steps descending into darkness. Without hesitation, she entered the landing and closed the door behind her, plunging herself into the gloomy unknown, trusting the spirits as she always had. Feeling her way along the wall, the stairway seemed to go deeper than the one that led into the sacred chamber. At the bottom, a single torch burned, unable to dispel the deep shadows that surrounded her. So far underground, Amira could no longer hear the cries of war and sounds of wanton destruction. She took the torch with thanks to the deities for their assistance in acquiring the scrolls, and began her trek down the uncharted tunnel.

"In the sacred chamber, the Triad Witches began to stir. You looked at each other without recognition and wondered what you were doing in this unknown place," concluded Maxine.

"The rest is a blur through time until now," said Cassandra.

"Where are the scrolls now?" asked Alexis.

"Helen and I believe they are somewhere in Victoria's shop. One of her minions tried to recruit us to join her coven. When we were in her apartment having dinner, we felt a strange vibration coming from below," said Sandy. "That's where you come in, Alexis."

"You will keep your appointment with Victoria at 7 pm. While there, try to discern the location of the scrolls," directed Helen.

"Is it wise for her to go alone?" worried Macy.

"Your concern is admirable. We don't want to arouse suspicion. It's risky enough with all of us being together. The energy field we're creating with all of us in one spot is like a beacon that can be seen for miles by one with the gift," cautioned Sandy.

"We will stay here and protect her with an energy shield. The combined force should be sufficient to repel Victoria's advances," said Helen.

"I had better get going," said Alexis.

12

Victoria's last customer of the day was leaving the shop as Alexis entered. She welcomed her and turned the *closed* signed over in the front window. Leading Alexis to the backroom, Victoria could feel a change in the young witch's energy.

"Have you been performing rituals today, my dear?" she probed.

"Actually I have in preparation for our meeting. I thought it was best to come cleansed and grounded so that I may be open to your teachings."

Alexis was tingling from the protection shield the others cast upon her. The rituals she had performed on her own made her more open to the energies around her. She could feel a strange pulsating vibration below her, but did not want to focus on it for fear that Victoria would pick up on it.

"You will be my best student. The others are not advanced enough to have thought of that on their own," complained Victoria.

"I've been at this for quite a while. It will just take time for them to catch on."

"You are very generous. When you meet them later this evening, maybe you can help me to assess their progress."

"Meet your other students? I thought this was a private session," Alexis grew concerned. Having the rest of Victoria's cronies here would make it more difficult to thwart any attack brandished against her.

Victoria peered at Alexis. Her energy field was much stronger than it had been earlier. It was exceedingly solid. She felt it to be a conglomeration as opposed to a singular force. Alexis caught the slight narrowing of Victoria's eyes. Was she being paranoid or was Victoria suspicious?

"Yes, initially we will be alone."

"Where do we begin?" Alexis attempted to distract Victoria from reading the protective shield around her.

"Since your attempts at calling forth spirits was a disaster, let's start there."

"I wasn't attempting to conjure spirits. I cast an abundance spell and they came," Alexis defended herself.

"Yes, an *abundance* of spirits." Victoria grinned. "I would bet money that you didn't take the time to cast a circle first. You must know the proper way to call and control an entity; to summon a particular spirit that can help you in times of need."

Knowing she was right, Alexis was quiet as Victoria began her instruction. Even in times long past, Mina's strong suit was not with the spirit realm.

"Since we have both done our preparation rituals before coming together this evening, we can jump right in," said Victoria. She selected an athame from several laid out on a cloth. The blade had a black handle. While it was not used for cutting during a ritual, this one looked as though it could inflict damage if that was the intent. Victoria pointed the athame to the northeast corner of the room.

"I cast this circle to protect us from all harm, and to contain all energy conjured therein." She slowly turned in a clockwise circle as she dragged the dagger through the air and enclosed the two of them in its protective fold. She faced north, raising her hands in the air, "I call the Watchers of the North and the Element of Earth to join us in our rite." Facing east, she cried, "I call the Watchers of the East and the Element of Air to join us in our rite." She continued clockwise, facing South and calling the Watchers and the Element of Fire, to the West, the Watchers and the Element of Water. Finally she asked for the god and goddess to join them. All protection was in place. Alexis watched, mesmerized, as Victoria put on a calm expression. She glowed with the energy of her work.

"I evoke and conjure thee, spirit of Qadir, in the name that is the highest of all names and at the command of the great fathers, you are ordered to appear before us!" She threw energy toward the center of the circle. A flash lit the floor and smoke rose from its heat. Alexis was horrified to see a rounded dome emerge from the tile. Its grayish bone color made it appear skeletal at first; yet as it rose, the form developed into a shroud-like being. More appalling still was to be in the presence of Qadir once again. Alexis never liked him or the energy he represented. To know that Victoria had been in touch with him all this time was unsettling, to say the least.

Fully manifested, Qadir stood in the center of the circle, looking at Alexis. "Mina, what a pleasant surprise," he said with an evil grin. "Amira told me you and your friends were in the area. We're hoping to get the coven back together."

Alexis was too startled to say anything.

"Together we shall pass through gateways yet to be explored, with the help of the Scrolls of the Four Winds. All of you need to be assembled once again in order for us to be able to tap into their powers," Qadir explained.

"If we had to be together to use their power, then why did you steal the scrolls in the first place?" Alexis questioned Victoria. She knew the scrolls were hidden in the basement of this very building. She could feel them pulsing. No other energy felt the same as that emitted by the scrolls.

"So, you have all come to remember your true identities. I knew my web had untangled, I just wasn't sure to what extent. It was the only way to find out if one person could wield the power. Besides, the three of you would never have agreed to using the power of the scrolls," said Victoria.

"We were trained to protect them, not to abuse their power! The magic we had and still have without the scrolls is beyond most people. What purpose could it serve? Besides, you have other students who could help you accomplish your despicable act," scolded Alexis.

"Qadir and I have continued our studies over the centuries. The scrolls cannot be controlled without representation for each direction. Others I have tried to train have proven unworthy of the task. The vibrational shift that is required to do the work is too stressful on the physical body and causes severe anomalies in most people. They know nothing of the scrolls or my true purpose for training them. Because we were born to the task, only the Coven of The Triad Witches is capable of such a feat," said Victoria proudly.

"We have read the energies of the scrolls, and it is possible to open mighty gateways and pass through them to experience worlds within worlds, the actual place that has been referred to in The Craft as 'a time out of time'. We could travel there together and accumulate powers far greater than what is possible on the physical plane," said Qadir.

"You're already a spirit. Can't you travel there in your present form, without the use of the scrolls?" Alexis asked.

"My spirit must be released from this plane in order to travel. I am bound to the Earth by my choices in life," said Qadir. "My visits are time-limited in this form."

"Join us, Mina. Convince the others to come together for this purpose. You will gain knowledge beyond anything you thought possible. This is the dream and goal of theurgists and mages for thousands of years. They did not know how to enter the gateways except through meditation and visualization. We will be the first to physically enter the gateway and to step beyond it," coaxed Victoria.

Alexis was tempted. It would be grand to experience such worlds, not for the power it would afford, but for the knowledge she would gain. Maybe the others would be willing just for the sake of learning. It might be possible to prevent Qadir and Amira from misuse of any of the new gifts that would result from the trips.

"There are four gateways that we have identified," continued Qadir. "There is one for each element: Earth, Air, Fire, and Water. We think there could be many more, but these are the ones that were most apparent. With each, there will be a specific set of teachings that can be derived. We are not sure if the experience will be the same or different for each one who crosses the threshold. All we know right now is that it will take the four Triad Witches to break through the veil that will allow us to enter the realm where the doors to each reside."

Victoria could hear the fatigue in Qadir's voice. She had to release her teacher back into the spirit realm. It would be a glorious day when he could be with her once again, without limit. "Qadir, you grow tired. We thank you for your time with us. I now dismiss you and all energies and spirits that have been attracted to this ritual. Go in peace."

Qadir lowered his head and closed his eyes. The form dissipated into tiny glimmering particles and vanished. The room was quiet, its energy lighter. Victoria released the circle and turned to Alexis. "Are you with us?"

The esoteric knowledge being offered was tempting. Alexis thrived on learning and wanted to comprehend the secrets of the universe. She could not speak for the others. "I am not in a position to decide. Give me some time to speak to the others and to think about all we have talked about."

"I have waited a very long time. My patience is thin." Before she could give a definitive answer, Ethan and Heather entered the room. "Alexis, meet Heather and Ethan."

Alexis looked at Ethan and was shocked to recognize him as the apparition in her bed. He smiled at her. "You look pretty good in clothes, but I think I like you better the other way."

Heather gave Alexis and Ethan an angry look. "You've been together?"

"No," Alexis said disapprovingly.

Heather peered at Ethan. "Then how do you know what she looks like without clothes on?"

"I visited her astrally. She didn't even know I was there," he said proudly.

"Have you ever visited me that way?" asked Heather, with hope in her voice.

"I wasn't asked to spy on you," Ethan said, still looking at Alexis.

Heather's jealousy rose. She could tell Ethan was attracted to this girl. He did not need instruction from Victoria to pay a visit to Heather's bedroom. If he were curious, he would have come on his own. She felt her anger building.

Alexis felt a tug on the protective shield that surrounded her. She saw a funnel of energy being pulled toward Heather. Victoria saw it as well.

"Heather, this is not the time," said Victoria.

Heather's fury blocked the sound of Victoria's voice. She had pictured that she and Ethan would be together, that he would show interest in her. How could he be so blatant in his attraction to Alexis when he didn't even know her? If she drained Alexis of her energy, Ethan would no longer desire her. She increased her pull on Alexis.

Alexis could feel her heart pounding and her head begin to ache. She felt queasy. In the distance, she could hear Victoria's voice reprimanding Heather. The room swam before her eyes as she tried to remain standing. In the distance, Ethan's voice floated by her ears as he scolded Heather. It was the last thing she heard before everything went dark.

* * *

The women were shocked at the sudden drain on the shield. They had watched the shield be vacuumed away. It was a startling technique, one for which they were not prepared. Sandy had been maintaining the energetic protection around Alexis at the time of the attack. The others felt the change and tried to intervene too late. Alexis was in trouble.

"We need to go over there and get her," said Helen.

"I'll go," said Macy.

"If anyone goes, it should be Helen and I," said Sandy. We've been there before. We can say that we decided to join the coven and get in that way. Tonight is when they have their regular meeting."

"The three of us can cover you from here," said Maxine.

* * *

"Heather, no!" yelled Ethan and grabbed her firmly from behind. He shook her until she emerged from the jealous rage. Alexis lay on the floor unconscious.

"Help me get her up," said Victoria. "Heather, you are a disappointment. I thought you had control over your gift."

Heather looked down at Alexis, at what her actions had produced. She felt only a tinge of remorse for how Victoria viewed her behavior and nothing more. She drained that girl and now Ethan would not want her anymore. Now he would see Heather's power and be attracted to her.

"Another episode like that, and you will be asked to leave. Your abilities are only to be used when and where I say," scolded Victoria.

Ethan's gaze held disapproval. He shook his head as he helped Victoria lift Alexis's limp body off the floor and onto a sofa. She reminded him of a ragdoll. He had not realized how dangerous Heather had become. Ethan never planned to have a relationship with Heather. He wanted to string her along, letting her think she had a chance. If they had actually become intimate, she might have killed Alexis rather than just draining her. Alexis breathed shallowly, her chest rising only slightly, but she was alive. Tormenting her was entertaining; killing her was unacceptable.

Heather's superiority lessened with the threat of being excommunicated from the group, her family. The thought of leaving them made her heart hurt. She still had no regret for thwarting her rival, yet she desperately needed Victoria and Ethan's approval. She vowed to herself that she would try harder to conduct herself the way they wanted her to. She hung her head to feign regret and said, "Yes ma'am."

Alexis's eyes fluttered. She was having difficulty fixing her gaze. Her head pounded in rhythm with her heart. She heard thumping as well, but was not sure where it was coming from. She saw a silhouette move across her line of sight, followed by low muttering.

Ethan went to see what the disturbance was in the showroom. Upon seeing Helen and Sandy, he had to think quickly and block their entrance to the back room.

"Hello, Ethan. We've decided to come to a meeting and possibly join the coven," said Sandy.

Ethan tried to look enthusiastic at their change of heart. "That's great, but tonight isn't good."

"I thought you said this is when you meet," said Helen.

"It is, but we were just in the middle of a complex ritual. The interruption caught everyone off-guard, and now they are a bit grumpy, not open to new recruits," he lied.

"Nonsense. We might be able to assist," said Sandy as she pushed her way past Ethan with Helen right behind her. They walked toward the back room. Ethan tried to block their approach. They could feel the scrolls, the vibration pulsating below them.

"Who is it?" called Victoria from the back room.

"Sandy and Helen, here to join the coven," replied Ethan. The two women continued to move toward the sound of Victoria's voice. Ethan gestured for them to stop and whispered, "One of our members passed out from the excitement, and we're trying to revive her."

"I can help with that!" Helen said enthusiastically and pressed past Ethan with Sandy in tow.

Victoria looked up from her ministration as they entered the room. "We heard there is someone in distress and are here to render assistance," said Helen. "What happened?"

Victoria stared at Ethan, displeased that he had let them in. "The smoke from the incense and candle fumes may have gotten to her. It happens sometimes," Victoria knew it was a meager fabrication.

"From the looks of her auric field, I'd say she needed a good dose of energy," offered Helen. "I am adept at energetic rejuvenation. Let me give it a try." Before Victoria could object, she wangled her way between Victoria and Alexis. Helen lifted Alexis's head and sat beneath it, placing it gently on her lap. She placed her hands on either side of her head, left-hand fingers pointing toward Alexis's feet and those on the right pointing in the opposite direction. Helen inhaled a deep breath. As she exhaled, Alexis was imbued with much-needed energy. It encased her head, then worked its way down her body to the tips of her toes. The energy field sparkled with silver light that moved into Alexis's physical body as it replenished her auric body. Helen sealed the energetic coating with a cobalt blue outline. Victoria's eyes narrowed as she saw the potent energetic elixir that now surrounded Alexis. Helen was no ordinary light worker. Helen released Alexis and moved away from the sofa. Alexis began to move and slowly sat up.

"Your vitality will return, just give yourself an opportunity to absorb the energy that has been restored," instructed Helen.

"I haven't seen such powerful healing since the old days, Huda" Victoria revealed her true identity.

"Thanks for the vote of confidence, Amira," Helen smirked. "In all the excitement, I guess we let our cloaks down."

"And let me guess, it's none other than Akilah," Victoria continued.

"Blessings to you, Amira," smiled Sandy.

Ethan and Heather were confused. They were not privy to the underlying meaning of the conversation. They looked to Victoria for an explanation.

"You know them?" said Ethan; incredulous that Victoria had not mentioned it before.

"These are some old colleagues of mine," she explained. "I haven't seen them in ages." Turning to the timeless teachers, Victoria asked, "Has the group reassembled?"

"You know it was inevitable despite your best attempts to keep us apart. The Watchers ensured that we stayed in proximity to our students, said Sandy. "I'm sure your teacher is someplace close by."

"He is, but in spirit form," said Alexis in a weak voice. She rubbed her head with closed eyes.

"I think we've all had enough for one night," said Helen. "If you insist on continuing this debacle, then let's do it in a civilized manner and congregate tomorrow for lunch."

"Fine, we can meet here," said Victoria, trying to regain control of the situation.

"Neutral ground," demanded Sandy.

"How about *Esca*. They have a private room for the gathering. I can call and arrange it," offered Ethan.

"That's fine," agreed Helen. "We'll see you there tomorrow at 1 pm." She and Sandy helped Alexis stand up and walked her slowly out the door to safety.

The three remaining witches watched them go. "I'm looking forward to the lunch and hearing all about what's going on," said Heather.

"You're not going, my dear. Neither are you, Ethan," said Victoria.

"How can you cut us out of this? Heather and I should be there," insisted Ethan. Heather gazed at him lovingly for including her.

"You may be arranging this gathering, but you will not attend. It is no place for novices," stated Victoria. "Just make the arrangements. I will provide information that is pertinent to you after the meeting." She turned away and began putting away her ritual tools, signaling the end of the conversation.

Ethan grabbed Heather's hand and led her out the door and into the night.

"Why won't she let us go with her?" asked Heather, hurt by the rejection.

"We can't go in physical form, but we will know everything that is happening," said Ethan confidently.

"But how?"

"Same way I was able to spy on Alexis," Ethan saw Heather bristle. "Calm down, I have no interest in her," he saw Heather's posture relax. "I can be there in astral form, listen to the conversation, then tell you what's going on."

Heather smiled. Ethan was making sure she was included. He leaned forward and kissed her gently on the lips, sending a tingle through her. "See you tomorrow," he said and walked down the street toward home. Heather stood still, basking in the warmth of the kiss, afraid that leaving that spot would dispel the magic Ethan bestowed upon her.

13

The Witches and their instructors arrived on time. It was a reunion. To have Amira with them was bittersweet. Those of the light forgave Amira for her transgressions and were ready to have an open conversation. Amira as Victoria arrived, walking into the room with trepidation. She felt singular in her purpose, no longer a part of the original coven. It surprised her to be welcomed and made to feel comfortable. The conversation was light and humorous, reminiscing about past adventures and follies. Victoria contributed some mild memories of her own that were met with delight from the others. She was careful to guard against deception, although she detected no such ruse. The room glowed with the chatter and enjoyment of old friends congregating.

Macy could see that the interaction was strained for Victoria. She tried to ease the tension. "Shall we call each other by our current names or our ancient ones?" she asked the group.

"Current names. That way we have started anew and can move forward from here, not forgetting about the past, but to acknowledge it, learn from it, and move beyond it," said Alexis, emphasizing her willingness to forgive and forget by looking over at Victoria.

Maxine nodded her approval. Her student was gracious and forgiving. "I agree," she chimed in.

The rest raised their glasses in agreement. Victoria raised hers halfway, still uncertain that she was once again part of the coven.

"Victoria," said Macy, "We know that you did not attack Alexis last night. She told us it was Heather."

"A novice," Victoria shook her head in dismay, "She has no control. That is the danger of training new recruits. They did not have the advantages that we had training from birth," she raised her glass higher and smiled.

The group mimicked her gesture with murmurs of "Here, here!"

"I never intended for anyone to be injured. Heather demonstrated that selfish motives are dangerous when misguided," Victoria admitted. She looked down at her mostly full plate.

"We can't control the actions of others; we can only be in command of our own behavior. Taking responsibility for what we do is the most important thing. Understanding the consequences of our actions and rectifying transgressions effectively neutralizes bad Karma," said Sandy.

"So true," Maxine joined in. "Everyone does things they regret. The marvelous thing is that while we cannot take it back or erase it, we can take another action to correct it that shows we have learned the lesson in the situation. While the original act is imprinted on the ether, so shall be all others. It is up to those affected by the initial act to recognize the motivation to resolve the malefaction and to allow new energy to come into the situation."

"It is my obligation then to put things right. The scrolls are safe for now, but we need to put them in a timeless hiding place. I ask for your help in that task," Victoria said.

Sandy watched Victoria's aura as she spoke. There were layers of color and texture, some well-intended, bright, and smooth; others were jagged and dark. The conflict within her was apparent, her spirit in constant struggle with her devotion to Qadir. Her remorse did not dilute his influence; he still held sway over her.

"What about Qadir and exploring the Gateways?" asked Alexis, as though reading Sandy's thoughts.

"Qadir has his own reasons for exploring other worlds. I've been thinking about their potential as well. The Gateways may be the perfect place to hide the scrolls, but we won't know unless we go there," said Victoria.

Sandy detected a modicum of sincerity in Victoria's statement, yet the dark layers persisted and muddied the light of the desire to make amends. The Gateways were spoken of in legend. None had attained entrance, yet many had seen the openings.

Cassandra spoke up. "What are the dangers of going through the Gateways?"

Always practical, thought Helen. She looked at Maxine. "You are best versed in the legend of the Gateways. What can you tell us?"

"The scrolls not only hold the balance of all celestial energies, but they are also the keys to the Elemental Gateways. Attempts at entering these sacred realms have been unsuccessful, as the efforts were made by individuals or by groups that were not adequately trained or prepared," said Maxine. "Because no one has actually accomplished the feat, we cannot be certain of what dangers lie ahead. This group, the coven of Triad Witches, is the best prepared and most likely to succeed in entering these worlds. You would be the first to pass through.

"The scrolls represent each direction, each elemental vibration. These vibrations are matched to the corresponding gateway. Using the scrolls alone will not grant access; the physical body must also be vibrating to that element and all it represents. Each of you was created with this in mind. Your parents were selected in accordance with their vibrational patterns, along with their knowledge. Your teachers were chosen to train you to act in accordance with the vibrational patterns of each element and direction. Your times of power, the colors and gemstones that you respond to, are all characteristic of the elemental forces of the scrolls and the gateways."

"So, this was our true purpose from the beginning. Not just to protect the scrolls, but to use them to unlock the mysteries of the Elemental Gateways," Macy said with astonishment.

"We can't be sure of what the dangers are, so we also don't know the benefits," thought Cassandra aloud.

"Not specifically, but it's certain that we would gain knowledge beyond the dearest dreams of all who have gone before us. To venture into the unknown and return to share the knowledge of those realms would be the benefit," said Alexis.

"Some things were never meant to be known," said Cassandra fearfully. "Not everyone has the same penchant for knowledge and the wisdom to use it for the common good as you do, Alexis."

"She's right," said Macy. "In sharing what we learn, there is a risk of abuse. The information will be extremely potent. In the wrong hands, it could cause irreparable damage to the known universe and all life within it."

"That's true of most knowledge. The most wondrous scientific discoveries had and have the potential for abuse. Genetic research produces both miraculous and detrimental results. The ability to alter the genetic structure of a life form has implications that impact the entire chain of existence," said Helen.

"If we were not meant to visit the World Between The Worlds, the Universal Energy would have ensured that it could not occur. Our very existence is testament to the validity of the goals of mystics through the ages. The desire to connect with the Universal Life Force through whatever means is inherent in the human species," Sandy said.

Maxine chimed in. "You were born for this purpose. The prophets foretold it. You are obligated to reveal that which is hidden, to pursue the occult and bring it to light through understanding."

"With our energies vibrating to the appropriate gateway, we will be safe. My guidance tells me that those who have tried to enter the gateway without appropriate preparation have gone insane in the process. The energies overwhelmed them and short-circuited the delicate balance within the physical form," Alexis felt certain she was correct.

Considering the risks and benefits of the journey, she called upon her guidance so that her personal desires did not get in the way. It always spoke the truth. It cut through the emotionality and laid bare the issue at hand. It had spoken to her throughout the night, urging her to pursue this mystifying adventure.

The group fell silent, pondering the arguments that had been brought forth. Victoria had been listening to all opinions without comment. Their bantering sufficiently exposed the pros and cons of the situation. Better they convince themselves than for her to manipulate them into it. Willing colleagues were effective participants. They would wholeheartedly share in the quest.

"Would you like to consult your guides and each other to further consider the implications of our task?" asked Victoria.

"I'm ready for a vote," said Alexis. The others nodded in agreement.

"How many vote *yes*, to conquer our fears and move forward in our quest for knowledge and completion of our purpose?" Alexis asked the group. "Show of hands."

There was a moment of hesitation, all the women looking to see what the others would do. Alexis put her right hand straight up in the air. Victoria's hand followed. The rest raised their hands slowly, still contemplating the enormity of what they were about to do. Consensus was total. They knew that they had come through time to fulfill their duty, the reason they were brought into this world.

"A plan is needed before we move forward. There is also much preparation that must take place to ready the four of you for your journey," instructed Sandy.

"You're not coming with us?" asked Cassandra, disappointment showing on her face.

"We will be here to ground you while you travel," assured Helen.

"Our energies will be with you to safeguard against calamity. If something goes awry, we will be there to retrieve you," confirmed Maxine.

Alexis was barely able to contain herself. This is the information she had waited lifetimes to attain.

"Let's reconvene at my house to formulate the plan," said Macy.

* * *

In the comfort of Macy's spacious abode, the conversation and planning continued. Timing was critical, and the veil between the worlds would be the thinnest on Halloween, only five days away. That was the prime time to access the gateways. It was decided that each Witch would travel to her corresponding gateway, anchored by her teacher. For Victoria, this would be more challenging, but not impossible. She would call Qadir from the ether realm rather than from the physical. In that way, he could accompany her through the Northern Gateway of the Element of Earth. She hoped he would cooperate and ensure her safety by staying on the outside of the portal, but she could not be certain of his willingness to collaborate rather than control.

The Watchers' rule of having the scrolls in close proximity to avoid celestial disaster was of concern. It was difficult to determine if the scrolls would be considered separated if each Witch held one of them on her journey. It was decided that because the Witches would carry only the energetic embodiment of the scrolls, the scrolls themselves would physically be in close proximity, and thereby satisfy the rule with no sinister effects.

Fasting would begin the following day, the Witches allowed to imbibe only pure juices and water until Halloween. Daily meditation and breathing exercises were mandated. Energy building movements, grounding and centering, and relaxation were part of the routine as well. Macy had taken a week off from work and Cassandra and Victoria closed their businesses to participate in this grand preparation. The better prepared they were physically, spiritually, and mentally, the more successful they would be in returning safely from the outer realms back to their own world.

Ethan filled Heather in as to what was happening. He had mixed emotions about being excluded from the adventure. It sounded extremely risky and as a beginner in this type of work, he did not feel prepared to accompany them on the journey. At the same time, he envied their abilities to travel beyond this world and to discover realms previously unknown to mankind. He would be waiting for their return to hear of their experiences and decide what to do with the information… maybe sell it for an incredible fortune. He would know better once he knew the nature of their observations. Heather did not mind that she was not asked to risk her life. She was content to commiserate with Ethan and have him all to herself. This was her opportunity to comfort him and show what a good companion she could be.

The week went by quickly, the Triad Witches working together once again as a team. It felt right to be together once again. Even Victoria felt the long empty void within her filled and revitalized by the camaraderie. The sense of power that they shared had not diminished over the centuries. It was exhilarating to perform the energy exercises and conjure the beam of light they were famous for.

*   *   *

Halloween had arrived, its festivities evident on the streets of New Hope. Patrons and pets in costume walked the streets, looking in shop windows and sampling the delectable fare of the eating establishments that lined Main Street. The ghost tour was in full throttle, ushering groups of thirty to the most haunted parts of town. The tour guides spoke of the history of the town and the earthbound apparitions that served as reminders of intense emotional circumstances.

The trick-or-treaters were out in droves, so the women needed to go to the most remote location that offered privacy to perform their task—Victoria's secret room in the basement of her building. The others were impressed by the soundproof qualities of the room and the mystical feel it had when all of the candles were lit. The scrolls sat in the center of the room, pulsating and reverberating with more energy than they had in centuries. The Triad Witches had reconvened and were welcomed by the Scrolls of the Four Winds.

Victoria had been reluctant to reveal her secret place, but it would get her to the gateway. She had consulted with Qadir about the plan, and he acquiesced, agreeing that it was the only way. Victoria was more comfortable with the process now that she knew Qadir was in agreement. At the same time, something was gnawing at her about his quick conformity to the plan. She had known him for centuries, and his demeanor regarding this voyage made her suspect he had plans of his own. Her anxiety built as she envisioned herself alone in the portal; with no one she could trust to save her should any problems arise. Her solitary journey continued, and she grew weary from shouldering the burden alone.

The group pulled large, plump cushions into the space and sat in a circle around the sacred vessel that held the scrolls. Each Witch sat next to her teacher in the appropriate compass direction, with the exception of Victoria, who would meet up with Qadir on the other side. Shadows from the candlelight went unnoticed, the women poised in concentration. Their meditation would last for an hour before venturing to the World Between The Worlds. They had created eight-by-ten inch images of Tattvic symbols. Originating in Tibet, these Yogic Tattvas represented the four elements plus spirit. Prithivi, embodying the energies of the element of Earth was drawn as a square and placed in front of Victoria. Vayu represented the element of Air as a circle and was positioned before Cassandra. Apas personified the element of Water shaped as a crescent moon and was located in front of Alexis. The triangle exemplified Fire, the element with which Macy was aligned. Akasha or Spirit would be held by the teachers during the journey to assist them in protecting the witches.

As they meditated, they drew on the energies emanating from the scrolls. The scrolls themselves would remain on the physical plane. The witches would take energetic incarnations of the scrolls with them on their journey to gain entrance through the corresponding gateways. Their intention during meditation was to acquire the scrolls' energy in the form of keys to unlock their respective targets, while maintaining the Tattvic symbol in their mind's eye.

Victoria was having difficulty concentrating, distracted by thoughts of Qadir. Her mind kept drifting to the dream she had the night before of a gray, wrinkled monster with wings. It chased her relentlessly through dimly lit, winding tunnels until she became exhausted and turned to confront it. The creature stood before her as she awaited its first move. It inhaled, and Victoria felt the breath pulling on her life force, sucking her energy. Panicked, she felt helpless as it drew her closer to death. Repulsed by the leathery skin and stench of the creature's breath, she tried to step back, away from its control. The pressure was agonizing; Victoria felt uncharacteristically powerless in the throes of the monster. She remembered thinking that maybe it was her time to pay for her indiscretions, that her selfish actions and lack of judgment had manifested this creature to administer retribution. Taking a deep breath, she awoke shaking and sweating, wondering if this was a premonition of what her journey into the netherworld would bring. She was not willing to let the dream dissuade her from the mission. Her commitment was unwavering. If she was to die this day in her efforts, so be it.

Victoria pulled herself back from the visions of her dream and refocused herself on the scrolls. She derived energy from the scrolls as well as from her sisters and was grateful for their support. Victoria was adept at instilling fear in others and was unaccustomed to the dread she now held in her heart. She focused on keeping Prithivi, the square, in the center of her thoughts. Nothing else existed around it, and soon she began to see clouds moving across the background of the floating shape. Her breath regulated, she could now pull the energy of the Scroll of the North Wind and shape the key she needed on her journey.

Alexis had hardly slept the night before in anticipation of crossing over. The circumstances were perfect for an unobstructed adventure with her teacher next to her and friends in all directions. Despite Victoria's deception, she was pleased at the reunion and the assistance of such a powerful witch. Forgiveness was the key to that relationship, and all that had gone before was put aside. It was not healthy to focus on the past; eyes toward the future created the reality they would live from here on out, and Alexis anticipated a joyous and exciting life hanging out with this group. The crescent moon glowed silver in her mind, solid and resolute. She filled the shape with the energy of the Scroll of the West Wind, its vitality blazing forth. Alexis was confident in her ability to enter the elemental gateway of Water.

Cassandra felt her peaceful center, starting her meditation in her beloved woods, surrounding herself with the green of the forest, allowing it to fill her with strength to accomplish her task. She trusted the protection the teachers would provide them and had no fear of what lay ahead. The symbol of a circle was easy to maintain focus on, her mind awash with corresponding meanings of completion, eternal cycles, protection, and equality, all concepts she believed in. Cassandra felt completely at ease, willing to accept whatever was to be revealed in the in-between realm. She called the Scroll of the East Wind to fill her and charge her symbol with its light. Intent steadfast on accomplishing the task of entering the gateway of Air, she pictured the key that would allow her entrance.

Macy's triangle was flaming red with the Element of Fire consuming her being. Feeling a disturbance in the energy of the mission, she anticipated a battle from an unknown source. She saw only darkness when she asked for guidance as to where it would originate. Macy trusted her impression of conflict, as it had served her well in her work environment. It was a bit unsettling not to know the nature of the trouble, but she would find out soon enough. She asked for the knowledge she needed to overcome the obstacle and to ensure everyone's safety, including her own. Macy vowed that whatever barrier she encountered would yield to her will. Confident in her power, she called the authority of the Scroll of the South Wind to fuel her strength and to open the Gateway of the Element of Fire.

Sandy, Maxine, and Helen watched the Witches' astral bodies take flight to the World Between The Worlds. Ethan grew tired of spying; nothing was happening that he could tell, so he withdrew to find Heather.

⚡ 14 ⚡

It felt like flying, like floating, like drifting, ascending, and crossing over all at the same time. Cassandra was mesmerized by the sensations of the journey. She moved fast and slow, gliding and taking quantum leaps through the ether. Trying to grow accustomed to moving around in this plane, Cassandra tested the movements of her hands and feet. Neither touched anything solid, and it was difficult to get her bearings. It was incredibly exciting and peaceful all at once; such conflicting feelings without the anxiety that normally comes with ambiguity. She centered herself on the circle and clutched the etheric key, willing herself toward the gateway.

Cassandra realized that the she was able to hold on to the key because she and it were formed on the same stuff. In this realm, she could interact with other etheric bodies, as she was one herself. It was odd to have her movements and actions feel similar to being on the physical plane. She attributed this to familiarity, her mind habitually perceiving the situation the way it always had.

Her expectations forged a preconceived notion of what the gateway would look like, appearing as two white pillars with a lintel across the top and the Tattvic symbol for Air, the circle, carved into the archway. As she neared the portal, no such vision appeared, only a change in density lured her closer to her target. She sensed that this was the opening and moved unhindered toward the gateway. There was no keyhole for her to insert the East Wind's energetic key, so she focused her attention on the key, making it beam toward the indentation in the endless field of energy that surrounded her. No sound touched her ears as she moved forward watching the shaft of tiny twinkling light particles being drawn toward the gateway. Their disperse pattern condensed as they approached the portal. The beam of light intensified, and Cassandra turned her eyes away from the brightness. With a final flash, the etheric doorway opened, beckoning her to enter.

Cassandra was in a place of total acceptance and was open to the experience. Her intellect released all preliminary expectations and allowed her mind to perceive this realm of Air. Thoughts and ideas came at her in a rush, revealing concepts both familiar and esoteric. She listened without judgment, attempting to comprehend the meaning of the messages. They came so fast, one right after the other. Her vision was through the mind, her eyes useless, unable to perceive. Watching the thoughts, she realized that the scrolls were made of this energy, conceived of Universal Mind, the written word not as important as its intent.

Cassandra's comprehension grew; the scrolls were created to establish Universal Law to enable the intellect to understand the spiritual word. These words consequently manifested in the material world. Without this awareness, the mind is oblivious to the truth. Not all can sense it. Not all sought these insights with an open mind. When the mind is closed, no doors can be opened, either in between the worlds or on the physical plane. Cassandra struggled not to analyze the information, but to take inventory of the wisdom to be imparted upon her return.

Awakening to the Universal Mind is the ultimate protection from demons and dark forces that plague mankind. Darkness is triggered by doubt, fear, and hatred. These are the true demons that take possession of people's spirits. From the darkness came the light, creating life and the start of all things. It is the refusal to see that plunges the world into shadows. Love, reassurance, faith, and trust are elements of the light that pushes away the darkness. A merciful and pure intent is necessary to expunge the plight that selfishness and ignorance produce. When darkness surrounds you, there is always a bit of light that shines upon the situation. Open to the light to be aware of the seeds of opportunity that lay dormant until they are observed. The light shining within longs to expand and be expressed. Darkness is not evil; it is out of the darkness that light is born. It is a time of undiluted potential.

As Cassandra suspended her logical mind, it was clear that intuition only comes to an uncluttered mind and is distracted by structure and limitation. *Information received intuitively allows newfound wisdom to be an expression of individuality. By opening to creative thought and instinctive perception, it is possible to move in irregular progressions to grow and achieve goals, traveling from one stage to the next, allowing for pauses along the way. When the mind is not ready, the will is unable to push forward, its momentum compromised by obstacles or lack of vision. The delays are necessary to address periods of weakness and to strengthen the resolve and understanding of the individual. Seemingly disparate components of your life come together to effectuate long-needed change and progress.*

Completion is possible when the mind frees itself to conceive of movement that is of the Divine Will, not simply a conception of individual will. They work together to balance thoughts and emotions, to construct purpose, and to focus on the task to the end. At times of weakness, it is necessary to withdraw into meditation to strengthen oneself and to hear the messages available through the Universal Mind or Higher Self.

Cassandra floated and spun slowly in space, supported by the ether, not feeling her body. She had become one with the Universal Mind. Her understanding was boundless, her desire to remain in this state infinite. With closed eyes, the messages continued to bombard her mind.

Pure intent, determining a goal, asking the Universe for what is desired, and following your instincts are essential to achieving all aspirations. Without purpose, without focus, nothing will transpire. All must be in balance to move in any direction. Imbalance creates harmful vibrational patterns that are not conducive to accomplishing one's goals. The individual will propels one forward of his or her own volition; yet fate has a hand as well; the mysterious forces of the universe, the Divine Will, open the door where one could not be seen by the five senses alone. We determine what will occur; the Universe determines how it will happen.

Critical thinking skills are to be developed, along with the creative mind. These abilities used along with the intuitive sense possessed by all allow the individual to be connected to the Universal Mind. Those who negate this natural ability will be lost. Learn to trust the thoughts and feelings that seem to emerge out of nowhere. These are the ideas that come from the Universal Mind, the Higher Self. Know them to be as accurate, if not more so, than those that come from within the depths of the mortal mind. The connection with All That Is is possible as a result of the consciousness that is the stuff everything is made of. It is in all things, all beings, all of nature. When atrocities are committed, they affect every being on the entire planet and in the vast universe, sending vibrations of war and hatred. Raise the vibration by monitoring your thoughts and actions to include positive ideas that are for good. Thoughts have substance and imprint on the world. Thoughts prompt actions, and choices are a function of the individual's conception of what is beneficial.

The Universal Mind does not seek to control, judge, or guide. You are free to think and act as you wish. These thoughts and actions are not without consequence, so choose wisely. Avoid inserting yourself into someone's path for your own benefit. Do not rescue those who seem downtrodden; rather help them to learn to be self-sufficient. Develop the young to think for themselves and not to follow blindly without questioning. Give people the opportunity to make decisions and learn their own lessons, for each follows a unique path in their current lifetime. What constitutes virtue is for the individual to decide. Teach each person to understand how making decisions based on their intuitive guidance allows right action, leading to health and happiness.

Imagination is the outgrowth of a fertile creative mind. The discoveries made in this way put one on the path to enlightenment. Each person has unique gifts that, when tapped into, develop the life path in a way that is enriching and rewarding. The key to finding your true self is by thinking in a way that is unique to the person you are and want to be. Going against the inimitable attributes inherent to the self is to suffer anger, frustration, and depression. Consider the views of others; yet, follow the guidance within for the final assessment. Creative forces find their way to you; to open to the energy is all that is necessary. A free mind is an open channel able to embrace thoughts and ideas formerly unavailable, inspiring movement beyond the current state of being. Be a conduit for the divine loving energy that surrounds you and believe in your ability to manifest that which you imagine.

Mental flexibility guards against stagnation and self-destruction. It maintains an open mind, free from obstacles and shields that prevent growth. Flexibility is characteristic of the wise person who acknowledges that there is always something to learn and an opportunity to change. Grow the mind beyond where it has been to branch out into realms yet to be explored. The brain must be exercised and opened with new knowledge. Thoughts affect health, actions, and emotions. Cleanse the mental body to remove the clutter and stagnant patterns and to release positive energy. The calm mind is that which is most open to the realms of magic and wisdom. To contemplate the nature of the universe, divinity, and human kind is to allow us to know ourselves in an intimate way. The honing of the mind is essential in order to reach our greatest potential and to stay healthy.

It all made sense. The energy spoke the truth. She felt it deep in the core of her being.

* * *

Alexis soared through the ether, her excitement propelling her. The intensity of the movement thrilled her to the core, increasing the exhilaration of the experience. She was launched from her seated position in Victoria's secret chamber, into this realm of inconceivable forms and textures. When casting her protective circle during ritual and saying the words that it was representing the World Between The Worlds, she did not envision this. Her mind struggled to wrap around what she was seeing. The shapes appearing to her were foreign to her eyes and incomprehensible to her mind. A reference point was eluding her, and there was nothing she could call forth to compare it to. She could not use the familiar material world as a point of reference for there was nothing in this world that existed in her world. The realization blossomed that these manifestations were the imprints of actions that transpired on the physical plane. Both worlds impacted each other; everything was connected.

The bizarre shapes distracted her from the task at hand, and she refocused her attention to find the gateway of the Element of Water. She clutched the energy of the Scroll of the West Wind and asked for guidance. Two figures with recognizable silhouettes appeared before her. They stood out, as they were the only forms that made sense to her limited grasp of this realm. As she drew closer, faces became apparent – the faces of her parents that had died years before. They were a welcome sight any time, but especially amidst the native beings of this plane made up of glyphs, lines, squiggles, and frequencies floating across her field of vision. The essence of her parents came clear and she felt them sending love and warmth to her. She smiled as they pointed the way to the portal. Communication was vibrational here; no words were necessary. She flowed toward the direction they recommended.

The frequencies came at her in layers, manifesting as noise to her senses. She hoped the reception would improve once she was through the gateway. A small spot emerged in the distance, its energy moving in waves across the doorway. She held up the etheric scroll and pointed it toward the rippling gate. Flashes of light burst open the path, and she glided through.

The layers of information persisted; Alexis strained to understand. It was not working. She felt herself becoming overwrought with the effort. This was not productive. She focused on the crescent moon, centering herself to a place of calm serenity. Gradually she was able to decipher the messages. It was as though they existed continuously and simultaneously. Disjointed intelligence came through, singular in their meaning yet inextricably connected. She chose what to attend to, trying to avoid confusion. Alexis suddenly knew that these messages were always there for anyone who wanted to hear them.

...a great force waiting to be expressed through creative potential. Attune to the Self and the environment in order to tap into your power. Each person has a natural ability that must be grown and developed. This effort cannot be forced. Ride the tide of power by aligning the

will, the Divine Will, and the personal gifts bestowed. Tapping into the Divine Will allows one to transcend limitations and move toward fulfillment.

Focus maintained on the higher aspects of life is rewarded with passion, aspiration, and personal creative force. Evolution toward self-fulfillment is the path of all. Attaining the full potential of the individual is possible when detachment from concepts, emotions, and possessions is achieved. Detachment removes limitation. Not all lessons are available to us or are able to be understood until the individual is ready to hear and accept the guidance. Remove obstacles to progress by flowing as water. A sense of renewal will follow.

Be receptive to the divine energy that is available to you and experience the emotional fulfillment that results. Preserve attained wisdom and remove false notions and information. Fill your body with pure energy and protect yourself from contamination that can come from external sources or internal negativity. Be the connection between the spiritual and the material, using the higher self and your intelligence. Hold within you the positive attributes of joy, knowledge, and health and pour out that which threatens to delay your growth. Discover your own true nature by clearing away all that is not truly who you are.

The rapid flow of knowledge was staggering, yet she maintained her attention to avoid missing anything. This is what she had waited for her whole life.

Emotions run deep within spurred on by life experience. Love and joy enrich; fear and hate limit. Emotional reactions reflect issues that must be addressed within the self. Maintain power by controlling your own reactions. The actions of others cannot be controlled, but your reaction can be. You are responsible for your feelings. Being overly sensitive creates limitations. Approach life from a centered position and see the world with a more objective eye.

Do not pollute the Emotional Body with negative emotions. Avoid taking on the negativity of others; it muddies this energetic layer. Set boundaries and be clear as to what is needed to make your will strong and to manifest your own desires rather than that of another. Trust your inner guidance to allow the flow toward appropriate action.

Allow energy to flow through the entire body and outward into the auric field to create a powerful force. Strength is at your disposal and can have both good and bad effects on circumstances and people. At times when there is an overabundance of energy, picture a calm lake and mirror its peaceful qualities. Go with the flow of life rather than fighting against it, anxiety will be reduced and new opportunities will open up before you. Be aware of the effect that negative thoughts, people, and emotions have on your health and on your general outlook. Foster kindness and blessings toward yourself and others. The tried and true pathways that you have encountered are not the only ones available to you. Create channels that provide alternatives and new directions for your desires to be realized.

Listen to the spirits of departed loved ones. Allow their messages to come forth and do not fear their spirit forms or the information they wish to impart. Remember them; yet do not cling to their energies. Let go of your need to keep them with you. This will lift their spirits to the light. If you have recently lost a loved one or have ended a relationship, give yourself time to mourn. Grief is a powerful teacher; the departure of a loved one or the ending of a situation creates a space, an opening to be filled with new and wonderful relationships and opportunities.

Alexis felt this last message was for her directly. While others could benefit from it, she had been wallowing in the loss of her parents for quite some time. She released her grief into the ether, finding it easier to overcome her limitations in this realm of direct manifestation.

⚂ 15 ⚂

The launch was not as smooth as Macy had anticipated. Leaving her body behind was disconcerting and she hesitated as she felt herself rising. Remembering the importance of the mission jolted her free and drove her toward the outer realms. Macy kept the triangle shape uppermost in her mind, trying not to think about getting back to her body. It was difficult to leave her rational mind behind and to focus on opening to the world that lay ahead. Realizing that courage was an issue here, she battled with herself to overcome the fear that she knew would create obstacles to successfully entering the Gateway of Fire. The fiery energy was the key to her courage, and she summoned all of her passion and resolve to help her confront whatever lay ahead. She had butterflies in the pit of her stomach, signaling an altercation of some kind. That sensation had served her well in a business environment, tipping her off to situations where a challenge could turn ugly.

Macy was adept at handling confrontation in a corporate environment, but inexperienced in supernatural affronts.

The monochromatic view was unsettling, and Macy was unable to get her bearings. She laughed at her attempts to apply concepts from the material world in the astral realm. Recalibrating her thoughts, she shifted into intuitive mode, asking to be taken to the portal. At once she was directed toward her goal, the scroll in her hand warming as she approached. Hidden forces pushed against her, ascending toward a flickering light that resembled flame, yet with the gauzy quality of fog. Its colors graduated from pale yellow to red, waving at her to follow its beacon.

Hope flowed through Macy, bringing with it the promise of happiness yet to be experienced. In all of her accomplishments and acquisitions, she had never felt fulfilled. There was always an emptiness left after the goal was achieved, a hole where there should have been pleasure and satisfaction. Hollow are aspirations that have no affect on the well-being of others. Maybe completing this mission was the true objective from which she would derive joy. It was not a solitary journey; it included her friends and held within it the balance of the material and ethereal worlds. This extreme trek was necessary for her wishes of contentment to come true.

The colors intensified as she drifted closer, now seeing that there were two wispy flames standing guard on either side of the portal. Between them a dense energy prevailed, as though an iron door was closed before her. The iridescent blaze strengthened, reminding Macy of the Scroll of the South Wind in her hand. With her thoughts, she directed the scroll's energy toward the portal. It glistened and sparkled against the mass of the doorway, eating away at it until the entrance was translucent. Macy stepped through without hesitation, knowing this is where she was meant to be. Waves of light surrounded her, billowing as the silk cloth along the walls of her ancient temple.

She was here to receive something of value for the good of all and to rekindle her inner passion. Macy felt the light of the Divine presence in this place. She closed her eyes and took in the enlightened guidance it offered. Her role became clear: the protector, the truth finder, to reveal the nature of disruptive forces, and using her power to motivate and transform. She was being called to defend against evil and detrimental influences. One in particular slammed into her mind—Qadir. His command of the dark spirits was cause for concern; his command of Victoria even more so. Control was not the answer. Macy realized that her adversary was not Victoria, but rather Qadir. His influence was strong, and she would need to sever his authority over Victoria and the spirit world.

Protection against his magic was essential to get close to him, but the usual methods were useless against his power. Direct confrontation would result in her destruction. It must be done in a way that caused no harm to anyone else. There must also be a way to heal the damage he had caused and give hope for the salvation of his soul. Macy listened to the Divine guidance. It counseled to accumulate the resiliency and fearlessness of her youth and to trust in the protection she would be afforded in combat with Qadir.

An object was approaching from off in the distance. It spun and glittered as it came closer. Macy recognized it as a dagger, but one that was unknown to the material plane. The dull gold finish gave it an antique look. She wondered how old this relic really was, but knew there would be no answer. Its craftsmanship did not reveal its origin, for the design was unlike any she had ever seen. A design with many twists and bends was melded to the thick handle wrapped in rough cord and coated with a clear substance that allowed her to securely grasp the blade as it whizzed by. The blade itself was affixed to three sets of three-dimensional interlocking circles. It was weighty but comfortable to hold. She practiced a few slices and jabs in the air.

The knife was created to destroy demons, and Qadir was the only demonic influence Macy anticipated in this World Between The Worlds. Trying to envision the confrontation, Macy could not see stabbing Qadir directly or without assistance. *Trust*, the word floated into her mind, not insisting, but simply guiding. It was easy to accept and her decision was to in fact trust the process. This was her calling, her purpose. A task that was long overdue was coming to fruition, and she would do whatever was necessary to succeed. Silhouettes appeared far off to her left. The shapes remained together for a few minutes, and then one moved away, leaving the other standing alone. Unsure of what she was seeing, a function of the realm she was in, or an actual occurrence, Macy fought the urge to analyze the vision.

Instead she withdrew into an open intuitive state, hoping to glean the wisdom and strength of the power of the realm of Fire. As it surged through her, doubt disappeared, replaced by certainty that the distant figures were Victoria and Qadir. Getting to them was another matter. Victoria had entered the portal, leaving Qadir outside to wait. Macy did not know the rules of moving through this sphere. Could she go straight from here or did she need to exit the gateway and find them from another vantage point?

Whispering to Victoria, she directed her voice toward her sister, hoping that Qadir would not hear. She shielded her voice in a mesh of energy, relying on its strength to prevent unwanted ears from listening. *Victoria, I am here. I see Qadir. What is your intention?* Macy received the fear and worry about Qadir, confirming that he must be removed from the situation. Exiting through the Gateway of Fire, Macy held the Scroll of the South Wind in her left hand, the demon dagger in her right. *I'm on my way, Victoria.*

* * *

With effortless attainment, Victoria found the Gateway of Earth. Her previous astral journeys had prepared her for this special adventure. Clutching the Scroll of the North Wind in her right hand, she squeezed it in her fist as she saw the form of Qadir waiting for her next to the portal. Her corporeal body tensed at his presence. There was something foreboding about his appearance, more threatening. She had always been wary of him, seeking to please the master that could destroy her with his powers. She continued to train, hoping that her knowledge would one day include the wherewithal to obliterate him, removing him from her life forever. His influence had led her to betray her sisters and move through the centuries in loneliness. He had convinced her that power was everything, that once she gained ultimate control over others, then she would feel whole.

In this realm, his motives became transparent. Realization washed over her; she had been used. He could not enter the gateway himself or he would not be standing outside of it. Concealed behind his grim smile and glowing dark eyes was the devastating truth. As her teacher, he led her, helping her to see how power was to be used for selfish gain. His lessons trembled in her mind along with the fists that sought revenge. She looked about, checking to see if he had called forth his dark army to assist him. There was nothing about, except the green glow of the portal before her. She felt healing coming from the doorway, the potential to regain her integrity and choose to wield her power on the side of benevolence. The real power was in her choices and the ability to assess for herself what constitutes right action.

Victoria knew she could reshape her world, to transcend the darkness and move beyond it. While the darkness was simply another aspect of reality, she could choose to use her knowledge of the shadows to bring forth light. This new path had been obstructed by the desires of Qadir. Her suffering could have been avoided but provided a valuable lesson. Operating in darkness had taken her off balance, destroying her emotional center. Her capacity for love and caring had diminished in the gloomy world of selfishness. She teetered on the borders of madness, having been guided by this demented sorcerer who thought only of himself. It was time to restore the balance.

She stood before Qadir, considering her next move. "Open the gateway, my dear," he coaxed her in a soothing tone that did not match his toxic expression.

"Once I do, then what?"

"I will wait out here and ensure your safe return," he promised. "You are the only one who can go through the portal and retrieve what is on the other side."

"And what is that, Qadir?"

"We cannot be sure until you are on the other side. I've been waiting to find out for a long time."

Uncertain of the situation with both Qadir and the portal, Victoria decided to enter the gateway, knowing he could not follow. She pointed the scroll at the portal and the edges glowed bright green. The center vanished and she stepped through. The other side was foggy green, a dim glow surrounding her. Her insecurity vanished, replaced by a grounded sense of stability and of hope. The energy in this realm comforted her. She felt forgiven and freed from the bondage imposed by Qadir. Her faith and strength returned to her; inner peace flooded her being and a renewed sense of clarity came upon her.

Victoria had envisioned her unlimited potential being used to conquer the material world, yet with her newfound introspection, she saw far beyond that mundane purpose. She felt worthy of her power and in control of her destiny. Connected to the energy around her, she could feel the energies of Alexis, Cassandra, and Macy, as they explored the other gateways. Macy came through the strongest, as though she was trying to contact her. Released from limitation, Victoria viewed Macy as her ally.

Her mind turned to Qadir waiting outside the gate. Fear rose within her, his illusion of control creeping back inside of her. The messages she received were for her learning and understanding. What could be in it for him, except his demise? Her resolve returned with her anger at being his pawn. Her former insignificance appalled her, especially masked in her own self-delusion. The desire for self-worth grew, her spirit aligning and harmonizing with the healing vibrations of the realm of Earth. The energy retrieved her lost aspects, integrating her personality with her desires, and allowing Victoria to finally become one with herself.

Despite feeling whole, she was not totally liberated from Qadir or the guilt she felt over her past indiscretions. Victoria knew that until she achieved self-acceptance, freedom would elude her. Redemption would be a function of balancing the elemental forces, of uniting the powers of her sisters once again. Optimism cast light across the darkness of remorse, and she celebrated her reunion with herself and her sisters. Her resolve would be the shield against anticipated attacks from Qadir upon her exit from this utopia.

She asked the cosmic consciousness for guidance to overcome Qadir so that she could move beyond the evil bestowed upon all he came in contact with. In answer, an object came hurtling toward her, slowing as it drew closer. She reached out and grabbed the shaft of a mighty spear. It seemed to be made out of ashwood. *From the World Ash, Yggdrasil.* She flipped through her mental files. Yggdrasil was the world tree connecting all worlds. The Norse god Odin had a javelin made of this wood. The myth says that this javelin has magic to always hit the target it is hurled against. This must be what Qadir was waiting for. He wanted the mythical spear and the power it contained to add to his extensive collection of magical implements and weapons.

Preventing him from obtaining the javelin would be difficult. If she brought it through the portal, he would be waiting, probably with a plan to take it from her. She wondered how far he would go to retrieve it from her. Would their centuries-long relationship make a difference? She doubted it. His trickery was clear to her now. She opened herself to receive guidance from this realm of Earth energy. A faint sound touched her ears; a whisper heard through the ether and not in her mind. *I'm here. I'll help you.* Macy? She sent back her worries about Qadir and her ability to safely leave the portal. Victoria heard Macy let her know she was on her way. Victoria peered out of the portal and could see Qadir standing in the mist, fists clenched. He had never been a patient man in life; why should his spirit be any different?

Qadir's expression changed as he saw Macy approaching the portal. Victoria sensed his energy change and aligned her sight to his perspective. She was relieved to see Macy, but afraid of what Qadir would do to her. His arms went up, a sudden flash burst, creating a disturbance in the shroud of fog and mist. Qadir had conjured the monster Victoria had seen in her dream. It was targeting Macy. She knew how deadly this demon was. With the ability to absorb Macy's life force, she had to interfere with its deadly intention. Qadir and Macy saw Victoria at the edge of the portal.

Stay where you are, conveyed Macy. She focused on the demon with its gray skin and webbed wings, the massive claws aching to tear into her. Macy tucked the scroll under her shirt against her heart chakra, allowing her to grip the dagger with both hands. She willed herself to soar faster through the mist, straight at the demon. The knife held out in front of her, she concentrated on the beast's solar plexus. Macy felt the demon pulling at her energy, sucking at her life force with terrible strength. She flowed with the monster's energy, increasing her speed toward the target. The Scroll of the South Wind burned against her chest. Macy embodied its flaming power and surrounded herself in a shield of fiery energy.

Macy heard Akilah in her mind instructing her to use the Maqlu text, the ancient Mesopotamian ritual to protect against and destroy evil sorcerers, whether living or dead. Macy shouted the spell as she flew toward the demon, Qadir standing behind it.

> *Rise, great gods, hear my lamenting,*
> *enforce my right, acknowledge my transformation!*
> *I have lay down at your feet and brought forth my lament:*
> *because Qadir has done wrong, he was keen to do that which is*
> *unclean, may he die; we shall live! May his magic, his witchcraft,*

*his poison be dissolved; Release us from his disgusting nature that he may dissolve in the wind!**

Qadir felt his power dissolving, the need to exert more effort to maintain the winged demon before him tremendous. Macy continued her forward assault, dagger pointing at the creature as it struggled to diminish her life force. Only feet away, Macy held the dagger straight out and plunged it into demon's core before it had the chance to swipe her with its razor sharp claws. Qadir was horrified as he saw the demon dissipate, distracted by the unearthly confrontation before him, Victoria saw her opportunity. She threw Odin's javelin at Qadir, trusting that the legends were true. Qadir felt the spear plunge into his chest, sharp pain radiating throughout his etheric body. In dark bursts and smoke, the sorcerer's form disintegrated, reuniting itself with the Universal Mind, a threat no longer.

The dagger and the spear floated before them in the mist. Victoria and Macy raced together and embraced, their trial over. Without discussion, Victoria picked up the javelin and threw it through the Gateway of Earth before it closed tight. Macy returned the dagger to the Gateway of Fire. They knew how to get them, god forbid they ever needed the magical tools in the future.

Hands clasped together, they returned to their material bodies and their circle of friends.

---

*Excerpt with modifications from *The Texts of the Maqlu Series In Conversion and First Plate of the Series Maqlu* Tallqvist's German translations of the Maqlu Series translated from the German into English by Ms. Bernadette H. Hyner of the German Department of Vanderbilt University, 1894.

⚡ 16 ⚡

The Triad Witches sat exhausted on the cushions, glad to be back in their physical bodies. Each had experienced deep insights and received messages that were meant personally for them. The World Between The Worlds was a realm of realization and wisdom. Ethan stood in the corner unseen, having returned a few minutes before at Heather's insistence. The teachers beamed at their students, proud of the work they had accomplished. Maxine rose to serve water to the journeyers, who gulped it with gusto.

Helen would perform energy sessions on them all once they rested a while longer and after she summarily dealt with Ethan for having the audacity to spy on them and the conceit to think they would not know. She made no indication that she was aware of his presence. He had heard way too much, although his inexperience rendered the knowledge insufficient to do anything with it. He lacked understanding and humility. Ego continued to contribute to his downfall.

The teachers had watched all that transpired in the outer realm. Astonished by the teamwork displayed by Victoria and Macy, they commended both and welcomed Victoria back to the fold of the Triad Witches. Victoria received the accolades with appreciation, feeling fully vindicated of her past crimes against the coven. Sadness surrounded her success at the loss of her teacher. Evil as he was, there was a void left by his absence.

Qadir had been her primary companion over the lonely centuries and the teacher with whom she was energetically connected. With his destruction, the cord that connected them since she was born was ripped away, leaving an open wound in her auric field. Sandy picked up on this and promised that from now on, all teachers would provide lessons to the four of them, without separation in teachings. This was amenable to all. The gaping hole in Victoria's aura would start to heal when Helen applied healing energy and would get smaller over time. The speed with which it healed would depend upon Victoria's ability to let go of the relationship with Qadir. It would take time.

Plans were made to write down all of the wisdom the Witches had brought back with them in a special volume that would be available to all who sought the path of righteousness. It would be bound with a design that encompassed all elemental forces and the organizing energies of Spirit, to become the new trademark symbol of the Triad Witches.

The Scrolls of the Four Winds would remain with their protectors for all time. The women would find a secure hiding place where they would be safe wherever they found themselves in the world. Their future journeys through time would be together, each taking a turn, choosing the location for their return into the material world. The last one remaining in the current lifetime would be charged with transporting the scrolls to their new resting place.

"Now, we have one last task to complete," said Maxine.

"Haven't we done enough for one day?" said Alexis in a drained tone.

"The teachers can handle this last one," offered Helen. "Victoria, you seem to have two rogue students that do not understand boundaries."

Ethan shrunk back, shocked that they knew of his presence.

"What do you suggest we do with them, Victoria?" asked Helen in a voice that directly mocked Ethan.

Victoria smiled, "Strip them of their meager abilities, of course."

Ethan was devastated. He had grown fond of his psychic talents and wished to keep them above all else. His former thoughts of control and power dissipated, replaced by dreams of maintaining his current state. He must get back to Heather and warn her. They must go where the Witches could not find them. Overhearing how they had conquered a powerful and experienced sorcerer, he knew that he and Heather had no chance against them. His astral body pulled back, returning to his physical shell.

At Ethan's apartment, Heather sat beside his body, watching over what she considered to be hers. He felt her desire enfold him, and he wished she would give it a break. Ethan's constant mind for sex had been minimized by Heather's persistence. He saw no way of breaking free of her as long as she had the power to drain his energy at will, the way she had done to Alexis.

"Heather, we're in trouble," he exclaimed.

"What do you mean?"

"Victoria has gone to their side, and we are now the enemy. They know about us. They know we have been spying on them and seek to remove our powers."

"They have to catch us first. If we pack right away, we can get moving before they find us," said Heather.

"Their power reaches beyond the immediate area. They would find us no matter where we ran. What if we offer to join forces with them?"

"What do they need us for? Besides, I almost killed Alexis over you," Heather sneered at Ethan.

"What if we find our own gateway? We can pass through it to safety."

"Do you know how to do that?" asked Heather.

"I listened to the others. We can follow their method." Ethan began instructing Heather on how they would journey to another realm beyond the earthly plane.

"I'm afraid," said Heather, her cowering posture returned.

"We'll be together. Isn't that what you wanted?"

"Of course, but I wanted our bodies to be together. Our spirit bodies are another story."

"We won't have time to prepare as they did. Hopefully it will work anyway. Get comfortable and close your eyes…"

A knock on the door disrupted their concentration. "Don't answer it," said Ethan.

"I don't want to be a spirit forever, Ethan," said Heather, standing to get the door.

"It will be fine," Ethan said to Heather's back, knowing he had lost his traveling partner.

Heather opened the door to Sandy and Helen. She could not look them in the eye, and backed away to let them in.

"Do you realize the damage you almost did to others? Have you considered the damage you're about to do to yourselves?" said Sandy.

Heather's head hung down. She had no answer for them. Her new family was gone, and she had nothing and no one.

"Where is Ethan?" asked Helen. Heather pointed to the door of the bedroom. Helen walked across the room and entered the bedroom without knocking.

Sandy looked at Heather. "We don't want to hurt you, but you cannot be trusted to use good judgment when it comes to your abilities. They must be removed." Without another word, Helen raised her hand above Heather's head and pulled at her auric layer, then at her inner energetic layers, until she was satisfied she had retrieved all of her psi-vamp qualities. Heather stood there, feeling stripped naked, yet more stable than before. Her need to take the energy from others was gone, leaving her with a fresh feeling and optimistic outlook.

"I feel so much better," Heather told Helen.

"Your energy is now balanced. You have the ability to generate your own energy now."

In the bedroom, Sandy confronted Ethan. "You've listened to us from the shadows, and still you have learned nothing."

Ethan stared at her, trying to think of a way out and away. He would be better off now that Heather had bailed out on him.

"To bring harm is not the goal, Ethan," Sandy explained in a reasonable voice. "We seek balance in the world; we try to help others by what we have learned."

"What good does that do? What's in it for you?" challenged Ethan.

Selfish to the end, thought Sandy. "The sense of feeling good within ourselves, knowing how to choose appropriately and take the right action. Wisdom and truth are the rewards. We operate from a position of gratitude, in hopes of raising the vibration of those around us."

Ethan looked at her, not able to relate to what she was saying. "Whatever you're going to do to me, just hurry up and do it. I can't stand the suspense." He did not make a move, knowing that escape was impossible.

Sandy sighed. "It won't hurt a bit," she assured him as she raised her hands and energetically tugged at his aura. He was stubbornly trying to hold on to what he had learned. Sandy neutralized his ability to see with his third eye and removed the memory of how to astral project. To regain his talents, he would have to earn them back, along with the wisdom to use them appropriately.

Ethan squeezed his eyelids shut as Sandy calmly worked on him. Her gentle energy engulfed him, making him feel a sense of peace that he had never felt on his own. Fatigued from the stress of fright, Ethan slowly opened his eyes, noticing he was unable to see Sandy's aura. Everything was back to normal. He felt the misery of loss, disappointed that his talents were gone. He'd have to face Macy in the office on Monday, without his powers, without his confidence, vulnerable to the world. At least he still had a job.

"It doesn't have to be that way, Ethan," Sandy comforted him.

"Why not? My powers are gone."

"You still have power. It's inside of you. You must seek to rediscover it in ways that do not include ego. Challenge yourself to take on a new perspective. You're at the beginning of a new life."

Ethan looked at the floor, frowning. It was more like being back in his old life than at the beginning of a new one. He had nothing to say.

Sandy knew he was a young soul. It would take him lifetimes to understand. She waved goodbye and walked out of the room. She spotted Heather, grinning and talking to Helen. At least one of them was on the path to understanding. Before departing, Sandy and Helen wished her well and encouraged her to get out into the world and form new relationships. Heather was pleased that they thought she could actually do that and looked forward to giving it a try with her new outlook. It felt possible. She no longer perceived others as a threat; her feet were planted firmly on the ground, her mental state was stable and open. With Sandy and Helen gone, she went to check on Ethan, who still sat crumpled on the floor.

"Are you okay?" she asked.

He said nothing, as he looked up at her. She beamed with a radiance she never before possessed. It was not like seeing as before, but more an awareness that she was happy.

"Everything will be fine. Don't be glum. We're better off. It was fun, but I never felt in control the way I do now."

Ethan looked back at the floor. Heather wondered what she had seen in him. The desire for him was gone; her thoughts were on the future.

"Let me know if you want to get together sometime," Heather said in a non-committal tone, as she headed toward the door. She left Ethan's apartment without looking back.

Back at Victoria's, Sandy and Helen had stopped to pick up Chinese food, and the women were indulging themselves with abandon. Food was a wonderful way to ground them after such an arduous etheric journey. The conversation was light and full of laughter. Victoria felt truly part of the Triad Witches, none of the old animosity limiting her happiness and the sense of camaraderie. The dining room glowed with the joy of success and friendship that passed between the coven members. No one was the high priestess. The lead would be taken by whoever had the most experience depending on the situation they faced.

The need to relax did not last long, as thoughts turned to more serious matters.

"You know, Odin's javelin made me remember Qadir's study that housed all of his magical implements," Victoria said.

"None of us were allowed to enter, only you," recalled Macy.

"Maybe we should take a trip and find out if it is still there," said Alexis, ever curious to discover new magical tools and workings.

"What are the chances of that?" asked Cassandra.

"The study was a cave-like structure. After going through the doorway at ground level, a tunnel led underground to Qadir's chamber. It's possible that it was forgotten and remained untouched all these years," offered Victoria.

"If all of those magical weapons and tools are still around, they need to be inventoried and secured," said Maxine.

Sandy and Helen agreed.

"Looks like I'll be taking more vacation time from work," laughed Macy.

They joined her in the laughter, releasing the tension and excitement felt toward the journey that lay before them. All could feel that their adventures had only just begun. They would prepare themselves to face whatever encounters the Universe deemed their services necessary. In the meantime, they would focus on enjoying a serene evening of good food, wine, and fond memories. After all was said and done, Macy, Cassandra, Victoria, and Alexis knew that the true magic in the world is conjured by love, gratitude, and the bonds of friendship.

About the Author

Diane Wing, M.A., is an author, teacher, personal transformation guide, and intuitive consultant. She is the founder of Wing Academy of Unfoldment and has a Master's degree in clinical psychology. Diane has been providing valuable insights for the highest good of her clients for over 27 years.

Diane is also the author of the books *The True Nature of Tarot: Your Path to Personal Empowerment* and *Thorne Manor...and Other Bizarre Tales*, a collection of short fiction.

Diane works with her clients to find their Inner Magick and to empower them to create the life they really want. Her website is www.ForestWitch.com.

Get Better Results by Increasing Your Psychic Sensitivity!

A Journey through Madness with Haunted People and Places

The reader enters a reality where the world only appears normal—underlying is a dark world of occult influence, dangerous beliefs, and fearsome energies.

These 7 page-turning tales appear in this collection:

Thorne Manor: Meet Heather, a woman trying to separate herself from an emotionally abusive ex-husband. While pursuing her dream of opening a business, she finds herself in an old, abandoned mansion that houses a sinister secret.

Guardian at the Gate: A demon with plans to take over the world is given a leadership makeover.

The Black Sheep: A troubled, clairaudient girl rejects her psycho-therapist when a new spirit begins to counsel her.

The Quiet Neighbors: A housewife's first attempt at witchcraft back-fires.

By Invitation Only: A grieving pet owner is visited by an unusual creature.

Dream State: A woman's dreams become deadly reality.

Good Riddance: A man's hatred for cats creates an unexpected result.

Learn more at www.DianeWingAuthor.com

A Mini-Anthology of Spine-Tingling Short Stories

Kick back and enjoy these short stories from Diane Wing, author of *Thorne Manor And Other Bizarre Tales* and *Coven: Scrolls of the Four Winds*.

Another Walk in the Park: A familiar walking path leads to a disturbing encounter in an unexpected realm.

Dark Hollow Road: A grieving sister searches for her brother on a road notorious for missing persons.

The Restaurant: An adventurous foodie couple are consumed by a life-changing meal when they explore the peculiar cuisine at a mysterious new restaurant.

Wrong Directions: Jealousy prompts a technological genius to conjure a diabolical solution to deal with unfaithful husbands.

Raves for *Trips to the Edge*

"Prepare yourself for some chilling late night indulgence: Diane Wing continues to serve up tasty, elegant tales of spiritual mayhem and revenge with a modern flare. It's all included - hair raising action, mystical quandaries, chilling surprises, karmic debts and unexpected twists of fate. A must read for all true lovers of the supernatural."

--M. Ashcraft, Oakland, California

"Diane Wing's stories lead you to one seemingly obvious conclusion, and then she throws a flaming curve ball you slowly recover from. She sucks me in and as soon as I think I have it figured out, she turns the story in an unexpected direction, leaving me with chills and the sense that the world is not always as it seems."

--Antoinette Brickhaus Philadelphia, PA

"Trips to the Edge is surely that! Visually mesmerizing and breathtaking. If Pink Floyd, the Grateful Dead, and Led Zeppelin wrote a book together, it would read like Trips to the Edge."

--Annette Sadelson, Baltimore, MD